"Uh-oh . . ."

There was a pile of ragged cloth strewn at the foot of the stairs, and more leading up the stairs like a trail. Ryce walked over and peered at the cloth. It was vaguely recognizable as having once been one of her father's socks.

"Oh, no . . . Tchaikovsky . . . Dad is going to be really mad!"

Tchaikovsky didn't care. He jumped up and snapped at the pile of sock in Ryce's hand and hung there, growling at the cloth as if it were a deadly enemy.

"We better clean this up," said Emily.

Ted nodded vigorously. "We have to hide the evidence."

Just then Chubby scurried up, a mangled piece of leather in her jaws. She dropped it in front of the kids and barked happily.

Ted peered at the leather, still slimy from the dog's mouth. "What is that?"

"What was it, more like it," said Ryce. "You know, I think it's part of Dad's golf bag . . ."

Beethoven's Puppies

Robert Tine

BOULEVARD BOOKS, NEW YORK

BEETHOVEN'S PUPPIES

A novel by Robert Tine, based on the Universal theatrical motion pictures
entitled "Beethoven," written by Edmond Dantes and Amy Holden Jones, and
"Beethoven's 2nd," written by Len Blum. Based on characters created by
Edmond Dantes and Amy Holden Jones.

A Boulevard Book / published by arrangement with
MCA Publishing Rights, a Division of MCA, Inc.

PRINTING HISTORY
Boulevard edition / May 1996

The Putnam Berkley World Wide Web site address is
http://www.berkley.com

ISBN: 1-57297-117-7

BOULEVARD
Boulevard Books are published by The Berkley Publishing Group,
200 Madison Avenue, New York, New York 10016.
BOULEVARD and its logo are trademarks
belonging to Berkley Publishing Corporation.

PRINTED IN THE UNITED STATES OF AMERICA

10   9   8   7   6   5   4   3

Beethoven's Puppies

Chapter One

THEY'RE BAD . . . THEY'RE GETTING BIGGER . . . THEY'RE Beethoven's puppies!

The four dogs—Dolly, Chubby, Tchaikovsky and Moe—were definitely beginning to take after their great big daddy. Like Beethoven, the puppies were wildly fond of the Newton family, particularly the children—Ryce, Ted and Emily—but they maintained their most dogged devotion for Mr. Newton.

When he was at home, all four puppies would bark and jump, following him from room to room, delighted that their best friend in all the world was there. The funny thing was, Mr. Newton didn't seem all that delighted to see the four little dogs or to have them with him, under his feet, constantly. He grumbled, he yelled, but the little dogs never gave up trying to be with their hero. They knew that, really, secretly, Mr. Newton was delighted by them, enthralled and altogether deeply in love.

After all, how could he not be? The four puppies were

very, very cute. They were brown-and-white balls of soft, fluffy fur, short, thick, stumpy legs, and big feet that they fell over all the time. They loved to play, running and barking and wrestling on the lawn.

When the children came home from school, the puppies would be beside themselves with delight. They would race around and *Yap! Yap!* in their funny little voices. Ryce, Ted and Emily could play with them for hours at a time and there was nothing the pups would rather do than cavort with the kids.

Beethoven and Missy, the proud parents of the four dogs, would watch their children—the human ones and the canine ones—fondly, delighted that they got on so well together. If one of the puppies played a little too hard or started to wander out of the yard of the Newtons' house, a single, commanding *Woof!* from Papa Beethoven would bring them up short.

During the day, when Mr. Newton was away at work and the children were in school, if Mrs. Newton was out, Beethoven was in command of the house. He and Missy would sit on the front porch, watching the property, making sure that no intruders got in, that the house was safe and sound.

The only trouble was, the real trouble was already inside the house: the four active, destructive puppies. As soon as all the humans were gone, Chubby, Dolly, Tchaikovsky and Moe would get busy wreaking havoc on the household.

The puppies were just at the age when they loved to chew on things, and their sharp little teeth and strong jaws could make short work of anything they chomped on. Each puppy had a preference.

Chubby loved to chew on leather—any shoe, belt or

handbag left within reach became fair game for the mischievous little pup.

Dolly liked to chew on wood—table legs, chairs, Ted's baseball bat—nothing made of wood was safe from her jaws.

Tchaikovsky was partial to socks. When no one was looking, he would sneak into the laundry room and burrow in the baskets of clean clothes looking for socks—in particular Mr. Newton's socks. It only took a few bites for him to reduce a pair of socks to a bundle of rags.

Moe had a taste for plastic. It didn't matter if it was a plastic trash can or one of Emily's dolls. Moe would crunch it up like it was candy.

All of this went on under the loving gaze of Beethoven and Missy. They didn't see anything wrong with the behavior of their offspring. After all, they were dogs—and to dogs, chewing things to the point of complete destruction was perfectly normal behavior.

The Newtons took a less understanding view of their activities. Actually, Ryce, Emily and Ted did not mind all that much, despite the fact that they lost toys and clothes to the puppies. The merits of the pups certainly were greater than their childish faults.

When the kids got home from school, they would find Beethoven and Missy on guard as usual; they'd leave their posts and come bounding down the steps barking in delight. Beethoven reared up on his hind legs, put his paws on Ryce's shoulders and licked her face, then he did the same thing to Ted.

But when Missy tried it on Emily, the littlest of the Newton children, she tipped right over and fell down on the grass. But that was fine with Missy. She just stood over the little girl and licked her while she giggled and squirmed on the ground.

Of course, that was only the beginning of the welcome the kids would receive. The instant they stepped inside the house, the puppies came scurrying as fast as they could. They came racing down the stairs, yipping and yapping, bouncing and jumping for joy.

The kids giggled and screamed and rolled around on the floor until their ribs hurt from laughing. It was Ryce who noticed it first that day . . .

She brushed aside a puppy or two and wiped a tear of laughter from her eyes, then she looked across the hall to the foot of the stairs. There was a pile of ragged cloth strewn there and more leading up the stairs like a trail. Ryce picked herself up, walked over and peered at the cloth. It was vaguely recognizable as having once been one of her father's socks.

"Uh-oh," she said as she picked it up. Tchaikovsky raced over and yapped at her, as if telling her, full of pride, that *he* was responsible for this mess.

"Oh, no . . . Tchaikovsky . . . Dad is going to be really mad!"

Tchaikovsky didn't care. He jumped up and snapped at the pile of sock in Ryce's hand and hung there, growling at the cloth as if it were a deadly enemy.

Ted and Emily had fended off the puppies and were staring at the trail of socks. Suddenly the two kids looked very solemn.

"We better clean this up," said Emily.

Ted nodded vigorously. "We have to hide the evidence."

Just then Chubby scurried up, a mangled piece of leather in her jaws. She dropped it in front of the kids and barked happily.

Ted peered at the leather, still slimy from the dog's mouth. "What is that?"

"What was it, more like it," said Ryce. "You know, I think it's part of Dad's golf bag."

"The *expensive* one?" Ted's jaw dropped.

"The one Mommy gave him for Christmas?"

They all remembered how, last Christmas, Mr. Newton had gotten the usual presents that dads always get—ties, aftershave, more ties, more aftershave—until he had opened his last present. He beamed delightedly at the beautiful leather bag. It was so beautiful, he declared, he would not use it! But it was nice to know it was there.

"Kind of comforting," he said dreamily.

Mrs. Newton explained to her puzzled children that their father's reaction was a golf thing. One day they would understand.

But almost every weekend since, they had caught their father admiring the bag, carrying it on his shoulder, carefully polishing the leather and muttering something about "The Augusta National . . ."

The awful reality of what Chubby had managed to accomplish did not take long to sink in.

"When Dad sees this, he's going to have a heart attack," said Ryce.

"Well," said Ted confidently, "we don't have to worry about the puppies. I mean, he wouldn't get rid of them . . . Would he?"

His two sisters stared at him as if he had just said something incredibly stupid.

"You know . . . ," he said after a moment's thought. "He just might."

All four puppies were now sitting at the children's feet, gazing up, their eyes bright and alert. They were trembling with pent-up energy and excitement, as if they wanted to shout, "What now! What are we going to do now! C'mon! C'mon! Let's play! Time's a-wasting!"

Ryce scowled at them. "What have you been getting up to? It's a good thing we found this before Mom and Dad did."

The puppies yipped and yapped: "Don't bother me with the details!" they were saying. "Let's go destroy something!"

"We better find everything they've ruined and hide it," said Ryce.

"What about the golf bag?" asked Emily.

Ted snatched up the piece of leather and stuffed it into his school knapsack. "Golf bag?" he said, his eyes wide and innocent. "What golf bag?"

Ryce took a more levelheaded view of the situation. "And how long before Dad notices? You can run, Ted, but you can't hide."

"Can you think of a better idea?"

"Hiding is good," chimed in Emily.

Ryce looked around at the wreckage and then down at the puppies. "Okay, let's straighten this place up before Mom gets home. Maybe with a little damage control we can get them off with a warning."

"It's worth a try," Ted agreed.

"Let's get started!" said Emily.

The kids sprang into action. The first thing they did was race around the house to see how much damage had actually been done. It did not take them long to figure out that four active, healthy puppies with sharp teeth and a lot of time on their paws could do a lot of damage. In addition to the socks and the golf bag, the puppies had destroyed two more pairs of shoes (both belonging to Mrs. Newton), a number of dolls (belonging to Emily), some video game cartridges (belonging to Ted) and an entire collection of CDs (belonging to Ryce).

"Well," said Ryce, looking over the wreckage, "it's bad, but it's not as bad as it could have been."

"It *isn't*?" asked Emily. "It sure looks pretty bad to me."

"Well," said Ted. "They didn't eat a piece of furniture or anything."

"They seemed to have decided that leather, plastic and cloth were their favorite foods." She peered down at Dolly. "I thought *you* liked to eat wood, Dolly?"

Dolly barked excitedly, delighted that she had been singled out for something. She didn't know what it was but it didn't matter!

"Is it possible we have one puppy who isn't a trouble-maker?" asked Ted. "One out of four. It's a start, I guess."

As Ted, Emily and Ryce started to clean up the house, the puppies followed the kids around, attacking new objects— they figured that if the kids were so interested in the old stuff they had chewed on, they would love to have some new things as well!

So, as well as harvesting the totally destroyed stuff, the kids had to make stops to pull objects from the puppies' mouths. The puppies, of course, thought this was a new and very funny variation on the game and so pulled back, growling as fiercely as they could.

All in all, the cleanup did not go as fast as it could have, but the kids managed to gather up all the ruined objects and hide them in the garage.

"What will we do when Mom starts wondering where her shoes are?" Emily asked.

"Or Dad can't find his socks?" put in Ted.

Ryce had secretly been dreading that question. "We . . ."

She shrugged her shoulders. "They're going to find out eventually—I say we just break it to them gently."

Emily shrugged. "What else can we do?"

Mrs. Newton got home a few minutes later. Missy and Beethoven and all the puppies were waiting for her on the lawn, and all six dogs frisked and gamboled about her, happy that she had come home at last.

They were so anxious to welcome her that they crowded around her, the puppies in particular getting under her feet. To make matters even more difficult, Mrs. Newton was carrying two big bags of groceries in her arms.

"Hey, guys, nice to see you too . . ." She stumbled a few feet toward the kitchen door. "Now get out of the way!"

They followed her right to the door, crowding around her ankles. "Move! I have to get my keys!"

She put down one grocery bag and started to look in her purse for her house keys—but the instant the bag touched the ground, four very inquisitive noses thrust themselves in, smelling the groceries—the meat, the cookies, the milk— all the good things! All of a sudden all four puppies decided they were famished! They started burrowing into the groceries like moles in soft earth.

"Hey! Wait! That's not for you!" Mrs. Newton bent down and tried to get the puppies out of the bag, while holding her purse and the other bag of groceries in her arm. She was leaning against the door, fighting the very persistent dogs, when, suddenly, Ted opened the door.

A split second later, Mrs. Newton, the contents of the two bags of groceries, as well as everything from her purse *and* four puppies *and* two fully grown Saint Bernards, were sprawled on the kitchen floor.

The puppies, of course, thought this was the best game

yet and started chasing cans as they rolled across the floor. Chubby dove for the steak Mrs. Newton had just bought and attacked the cellophane wrapper with those pointy teeth. Beethoven gave Mrs. Newton a nice, big, wet, lick across the face.

Ted gaped at his mother. "Hi, Mom," he said. "Need any help?"

"What do you think, Ted?"

Ted thought this was probably not the best time to tell his mother about the mischief the puppies had been up to.

Chapter Two

MRS. NEWTON WAS GENERALLY AN EASYGOING PERSON, not prone to getting upset and capable of keeping her head when her husband, who was, as they say, excitable, was losing his. The incident in the kitchen didn't bother her all that much and the kids did assist in picking up all the groceries. They even managed to get the steak away from Chubby before too much damage was done to it. Mrs. Newton examined the little bite marks in the meat.

"Hmmmm," she said. "This was supposed to be our dinner. I won't say anything if you guys don't."

"Our lips are sealed," said Ryce, speaking for all of them. There was no need to say who they weren't going to say anything to. It was obvious it was Mr. Newton—all four of them knew that he would bust a gasket if he knew he was eating a dinner that had been tasted by Chubby first.

"Good," said Mrs. Newton. "That's settled."

She turned away and started to get busy preparing dinner. She was setting out the ingredients and getting the pots and pans together, humming to herself, when she paused and shivered. She had the very distinct impression that she was being watched.

Mrs. Newton turned around slowly and discovered that her three children were standing there, staring at her intently. There were as still as statues and the effect was slightly unnerving.

"Uh . . . yes?" she asked.

Emily looked to Ted who looked to Ryce—she took a deep breath. "Mom, what if something bad happened that wasn't really anyone's fault except that it turned out to look as if it *was* someone's fault, but not really."

"And not ours," put in Ted quickly.

"Really," Emily added emphatically.

Mrs. Newton squinted at her three children. "How's that again?"

"It's just that we're afraid of what might happen when Dad gets mad about this thing that happened."

"This bad thing?" said Mrs. Newton.

All three kids nodded vigorously.

"This bad thing that isn't anyone's fault?"

"Correct," said Ryce.

"You've hit the nail on the head, Mom," said Ted.

"That's good to know," said Mrs. Newton. "Except I don't have the slightest idea what you are talking about."

"Anyway," said Emily. "It's simple. Just make sure Dad doesn't get mad and everything will be fine. See?"

"Honestly? No."

"What Emily is trying to say," said Ryce, "is that something really bad happened and Dad is gonna get mad—"

"But we don't want Dad to get rid of the puppies," said Ted.

Mrs. Newton sank down into a kitchen chair. "The puppies . . . Oh, no . . . ," she whispered. "What have they done now?"

The three children exchanged worried glances. "Well," said Ryce. "Remember my CD collection . . . ?"

"And my dolls?" asked Emily.

"And my video games?" put in Ted.

"Yes," said Mrs. Newton, still mystified. "What about them?"

"The puppies ate them," said Emily.

"All of them," said Ryce.

"Gee," said Mrs. Newton. "That's too bad . . . But I have to admit that I'm relieved. I'm sorry that your toys are broken, but you don't seem to be upset by it . . . And if you guys don't mind having to replace them out of your allowance then, well"—she shrugged—"that's life."

"You're not mad?" asked Ted.

"No. But you really had me worried. That was some buildup to not much of a problem. I was scared."

Emily wanted more reassurance. "And Dad won't be mad . . . ?"

"Well," said Mrs. Newton, "seeing as he's always complaining about the noise from the CDs, the video games hogging the TV and a bathtub clogged with dolls, I think he's going to be delighted."

The three children seemed to relax a little. Mrs. Newton went back to her cooking, but the children did not move.

"Is there something else?" Mrs. Newton asked.

"Ummmm . . . ," said Ryce uncertainly. "What if—just what if—they actually managed to destroy something that Dad wouldn't be so happy about?"

"Uh-oh," said Mrs. Newton. "What did they get?"

"A pair of your shoes," said Ryce. "Honestly—two pairs."

"Oh, no," said Mrs. Newton, crestfallen.

"And some of Dad's socks," said Emily.

"Oh, no!"

"And this," said Ted, producing the badly mangled piece of leather from behind his back.

"Oh—what is that?"

"It's part of the golf bag."

"Golf bag?" It took a moment for the information to sink in, but when it did, Mrs. Newton felt as if she had been hit on the head with a hammer. "The *expensive* golf bag? Daddy's expensive I'm-going-to-the-Augusta-National-with-this-baby golf bag?"

The three children nodded solemnly.

"Oh *no!*"

"Well," said Emily in a very small voice. "Look on the bright side . . ."

Ted and Ryce looked at their sister in disbelief. Neither of them had ever imagined that there was a bright side.

"No one ate a piece of furniture . . . You said so yourself."

For the rest of the afternoon, the mood in the Newton household was somber and subdued, as if the kids and their Mom were waiting for a terrible storm to break.

Beethoven and Missy could tell that there was something up, that things were not as happy in the Newton household as they ought to have been. The puppies, of course, were oblivious to the trouble and continued to frolic happily, cavorting with one another as if they did not have a care in the world.

All of the Newtons, Mrs. Newton included, tried to go

about their business as usual, each of them, though, keeping an ear cocked for the sound of Mr. Newton returning home. A little after five o'clock they heard the sound of the car coming up the driveway followed a moment later by the sound of the car door slamming.

"He's here," whispered Ted.

"Stay calm, everybody," Mrs. Newton cautioned, though she was feeling far from calm herself.

Mr. Newton's key clicked in the lock and the door swung open. "Hey, everybody, I'm—"

He stopped dead in his tracks, amazed to see his entire family standing in the hall waiting for him.

"Hello, darling," said Mrs. Newton, stepping forward and kissing her husband. All three kids threw their arms around their father.

"Daddy!"

"Dad!"

"Daddy!"

Mr. Newton stumbled a little under all the weight he was holding up and he was mystified by this sudden deluge of affectionate attention from his family. More often than not, when he got home, Royce was in her room playing music and talking on the phone. Ted was glued to the TV and his video games and Emily was playing with her toys. Mrs. Newton was usually in the kitchen preparing dinner, but tonight he could tell by the aroma wafting out that dinner had been prepared already.

"It's not my birthday," said Mr. Newton. "Is it?"

"No, dear," said Mrs. Newton. "We can be nice to you, can't we?"

"Sure," said Mr. Newton uncertainly. "It's just that it's so . . . unexpected."

"Dear, why don't you go into the den and relax while I get you a nice cold drink?"

"Okay . . ." Mr. Newton took a step toward down the hall, then stopped. "Wait. There's something strange here . . ."

Mrs. Newton and the kids held their breath.

"Something's missing . . ." He turned his gaze on his family. "Something that usually—" Then it was as if a lightbulb went on over his head. "Where are the dogs?"

"Dogs?" said Emily. "What dogs?"

"Uh-oh," said Ted.

"That's what's different—usually, the only attention I get when I walk in the door is from all those darn dogs. Today, they're not here and you are. That means something is up. And I'm beginning to worry . . ."

"As long as you don't get mad," said Emily.

Ted clapped his hand over his sister's mouth. "Pay no attention to her. She's delirious and historical."

Mr. Newton's face darkened. "Mad, Emily? . . . Tell me what I shouldn't get mad about, honey."

Mrs. Newton knew she had to talk fast. "Now, honey, you should know that we had a little mishap here today, but it's nothing that can't be put right."

"And it was nobody's fault," said Ryce.

"Really," said Ted. "Honestly."

Mr. Newton crossed his arms on his chest. "Okay. What's going on? I want some facts and I want them now."

"It's the puppies," said Mrs. Newton. "They got hold of some things that shouldn't have been left lying around, and they chewed them up." She shrugged. "We're all sorry, but it isn't the end of the world."

"But it was the end of—what?"

"Some of your socks," said Ryce. "Mom's shoes and some things of ours."

Mr. Newton nodded. It was obvious to all of them that he was attempting to control his anger. "Okay . . . I guess I can live with that."

"And one other thing," said Mrs. Newton. "I'm afraid one of them got hold of your golf bag."

No one was prepared for what happened next.

Instead of going red in the face and exploding into screams and yells, Mr. Newton's face seemed to collapse, his shoulders slumped and he looked very, very sad. "I . . . I . . . I could use that cold drink," he said, his voice weary and downhearted.

"Of course, honey." She hurried off to the kitchen.

The kids took their father by the hand and walked him toward the den.

"We're really sorry, Dad," said Ryce. "The puppies didn't know they were doing anything wrong."

Mr. Newton nodded slowly. "I know . . . It's just that I loved that bag. It was so special to me."

"We know," said Ted. "And we're going to save up and get you another one. It'll take a year or two, but—"

"Thanks, Ted."

Emily gave her father a big hug. "We're sorry, Daddy."

Her father smoothed her hair. "That's okay, honey. Some things are more important than golf bags."

Emily nodded vigorously. "I know exactly what you mean, Daddy. Puppies are more important than golf bags."

"Well . . . That's not quite what I meant, honey." Mr. Newton sounded terribly sad—so sad that Ryce felt tears come to her eyes.

"This is awful," Ryce whispered to Ted.

"I know. I like it better when he gets mad," said Ted.

"He's breaking my heart," said Ryce.

Mrs. Newton returned with a tall glass of ice tea. She looked very concerned for her husband, knowing that his angry explosions were far less serious than this sadness. "Here you go, dear. Sit down and make yourself comfortable . . ."

"Thank you." Mr. Newton lowered himself into his favorite armchair. As soon as he was settled, though, there was a loud crack!

"Ahhhhh!" Mr. Newton let out a loud scream.

Suddenly, the four wooden legs of the armchair crumbled, the chair turned over backward and Mr. Newton was thrown sprawling to the floor. As he fell, he dumped the entire glass of ice tea over his head.

Ryce figured out immediately what had happened. "Oh no! Dolly chewed through the wooden legs of Dad's chair!"

"They really did eat a piece of furniture," said Ted sadly. He had the definite feeling that the puppies were going to be gotten rid of for sure.

Chapter Three

IN A SPLIT SECOND, THE OLD MR. NEWTON CAME ROARING back—he was on his back and he was really roaring!

Mr. Newton screamed and yelled and carried on something terrible for the better part of half an hour, storming around the house, still in his ice tea–drenched clothes, bellowing threats and vowing that all four puppies were out of their life forever! He raged and thundered so loudly that Mrs. Newton was sure that the neighbors could hear him; the kids took cover, and out in the garage, Missy and Beethoven and their children huddled together wondering what could possibly be going on.

"This time I mean it!" Mr. Newton stormed. "They are destructive, they are disobedient, they are—" Mr. Newton blustered and gasped, trying to think of the worst thing he could possibly call the puppies. Finally he found the exact words to express his rage. *"They are nothing but golf bag destroyers!"*

Mrs. Newton knew that she had to calm her husband

down, that he wouldn't see reason until he stopped yelling.

"Honey, why don't you try to relax?"

"Relax? Relax! How can I relax when I'm surrounded by dogs? How can I relax when I'm surrounded by dogs and by *dog lovers*! My whole family has turned against me! That's what's happened."

"Honey," said Mrs. Newton soothingly. "Why don't I get you another cold drink? A colder, *stronger* drink."

"That would be nice, but it won't make any difference," said Mr. Newton emphatically. "My mind is made up. The puppies have to go!"

"Daddy!" Emily yelped. "No!"

"Please, Dad," Ryce pleaded. "It won't happen again. We all promise it won't happen again, don't we?"

"Absolutely!" said Ted.

"Look, apart from the fact that they are as destructive as pack of Huns, it doesn't make any sense for a family to have more dogs in it than humans, does it?" Mr. Newton glared at his children. "How many of your friends have six dogs?" How many have a dog at all? If you want six of anything you can have six goldfish."

"Some of them have dogs," said Ryce.

"Six of them?"

"No," Ryce admitted.

"Then you see my point."

"Honey," said Mrs. Newton, "the dogs are part of the family. We love them and they love us."

"Would you get rid of one of us?" Emily demanded.

"No, of course. But—"

"Then you see *my* point!" said Emily triumphantly.

"I'm sorry, but the puppies have to go! And that's final!"

Mr. Newton had said this many times before, but the kids had the feeling that this time he really did mean it.

*   *   *

When Mr. Newton went out to pick up his paper Saturday morning, he didn't look at the front page or the sports or the comics. Instead, he turned directly to the classified advertisement section. He ran his eye down the column and then smiled broadly.

"Ahh! There it is!"

Every Saturday the local newspaper printed a list of animals up for adoption, free of charge, and today the puppies were in it. Feeling better than he had in a long time, Mr. Newton went inside to his breakfast and coffee.

As he sat at the kitchen table, his children came in one by one.

"Hi, Mom."

"Hi, Ryce."

"Morning, honey," said Mr. Newton to Ryce.

In return, all Mr. Newton got was an angry glare. Ryce got a piece of toast and went outside.

"That wasn't very nice," Mr. Newton said to his wife.

"You're getting rid of the puppies. What did you expect? A kiss and a hug? Get real, honey."

"It's for their own good," said Mr. Newton, turning back to his newspaper. "Why can't they understand that?"

Ted walked through the kitchen without so much as glance at his father. He poured a glass of milk and went outside with Ryce.

Emily came in, stuck out her tongue at her father and left.

"How long is this going to last?"

Mrs. Newton thought for a moment. "Not too long. It should all be over by the time Emily goes to college."

"Very funny," said Mr. Newton. Then the phone started to ring.

To Mr. Newton's surprise there were a lot of people who

really wanted purebred Saint Bernard puppies. The very first caller offered to take all four.

"All four? Are you sure?"

The man on the phone chuckled. "Mister, there aren't a lot of people around willing to part with animals like that. After all, they're worth about a thousand bucks each."

"They what!"

"It's mighty kind of you to give them away like that."

Mr. Newton hung up feeling sick to his stomach. "Did you know those dogs were worth a thousand dollars each?" he asked his wife.

Mrs. Newton looked out the window and watched as the puppies played with Ted and Emily. Ryce sat on the grass, with Beethoven's huge head in her lap. The kids looked so happy; she could hear Emily laughing.

"If you ask me, they're worth a lot more than that."

The first person to actually come look at the dogs arrived in the middle of the morning. He was a wiry, sour-looking man who drove a beat-up pickup truck.

The children did not like the look of him one bit. He hardly glanced at the dogs. "Just gimme any ol' one," he said, tightlipped. "Got me a junkyard and I need a big dog to protect the place." He glanced over at Beethoven. "I'll take the big fellow too if you want . . ."

Mr. Newton could feel his children's eyes boring into his back. "I . . . uh, don't think you'll find that these dogs are suitable?"

"How come?"

"They're very friendly," said Emily. "They wouldn't hurt a flea. People will steal all your junk."

"You don't understand, little girl, everybody is afraid of a big dog." He smiled and showed a lot of broken teeth.

"Besides, I'll figure out how to make him mean." He reached down and picked up a puppy—it was Moe—and held the dog up by the loose skin on the scruff of his neck.

"This one looks like he could learn to be mean."

Both Beethoven and Missy started to growl.

"Yep. He'll do."

Beethoven and Missy got to their feet, growling louder this time. The fur was ruffling on their backs and their eyes were yellow with anger.

"So, I'll be going now," said the junk man. He still held Moe by his fur and he was no more careful with the pup than he would have been with a paper bag.

All of a sudden, Missy and Beethoven sprung into action. Missy snatched Moe from the man's hand and Beethoven rose up on his hind legs and snarled, looking so angry and vicious, even the Newtons were frightened.

"Hey!" the man shouted. "What's going on here?"

"I don't think you met with Beethoven's approval," said Ryce. "I'm afraid your adoption application has been denied."

"You people are crazy!"

Beethoven was still growling, his head down as if he were just a split second away from attacking.

"Sir," said Mr. Newton. "I owe you an apology. There's been a mistake. I guess the puppies aren't available after all."

"Well, why didn't you just come out and say it?"

"I'm sorry we wasted your time."

The junk man just snorted and walked to his truck. Without a backward glance, he drove away.

"Daddy!" shouted Emily. "Did you mean it? The puppies can stay?"

"It's either that or Beethoven is going to kill somebody," said Ryce, laughing out loud.

Mr. Newton did not look happy. "I hope that these puppies turn out to be cheaper than a lawsuit."

The three kids hugged their father. "Don't worry, Dad," said Ted. "We'll take care of them."

"You say that now, but you can't watch them every minute of every day. It's only a matter of time before they destroy something else."

"What are we going to do?" asked Ryce.

Mr. Newton shook his head slowly. "I don't know . . ."

Emily spoke up. "How about obedience school?" she said.

Chapter Four

FIRST THING MONDAY MORNING, MRS. NEWTON LOADED THE four puppies into her car and drove to Edith Sitwell's School for Pliant Puppies. The proprietor, Mrs. Sitwell, was a tall, stern-looking woman with her hair tied in a tight bun—she did not appear to be the kind of person who wasted a lot of time smiling or laughing.

She looked over the puppies like a drill sergeant examining new recruits. "I take my job very seriously, Mrs. Newton," she said. "Anything your dogs learn here must be reinforced at home. Do you understand?"

Mrs. Newton nodded quickly. "Of course."

"Do you have children?"

"Uh . . . yes."

Mrs. Sitwell clicked her tongue and shook her head. "That's bad. Children are not disciplined. They allow dogs to get away with things that I do not permit." She glared at Mrs. Newton. "They have been known to give dogs treats—*treats that the doggies have not earned!*"

"That's terrible . . . ," said Mrs. Newton, thinking of all the cookies, potato chips and candy bars that had been given to her dogs over the years. "However, my children are extremely well behaved and do exactly as they are told."

"Really?" Mrs. Sitwell did not sound as if she believed one word of it. "We shall see about that." She took the four leashes. "Come along, doggies."

All four dogs sat down and refused to move.

"Oh, dear," said Mrs. Sitwell indignantly. "I fear this will be a *very* difficult case."

The phone was ringing when Mrs. Newton got home.

"Mrs. Newton? This is Mrs. Sitwell."

"Yes Mrs. Sitwell. What can I do for you?"

"You can come and collect your puppies at once!"

"But—"

"They are not now, nor shall they ever be, disciplined! I have never known such disobedient doggies. They are not Pliant Puppy material!"

"What did they do?"

"What *didn't* they do, Mrs. Newton! They have made a shambles of my academy! Come and get them at once so we can put this disagreeable incident behind us!"

"So what are we going to do?" George Newton asked his family. They were assembled in the den. The dogs were outside, unaware that once again their fate was being decided.

"Well," said Ryce. "Let's examine our options."

"Getting rid of the puppies," said Mr. Newton.

"Daddy!" Emily cried out.

"Honey, Ryce said we should examine our options and all I'm saying is that getting rid of them is an option."

"But not a good one," said Emily.

"We could try and train them," said Ted.

"That's an idea," said Ryce. "We could buy a book and learn how to do it ourselves, couldn't we?"

Alice Newton shook her head. "I met Mrs. Sitwell; you didn't. Believe me, if she can't do it, we can't either."

"Well, they're not going to train themselves," said Mr. Newton. "Something has to be done and it has to be done soon."

"Wait," said Ted. "I have an idea." He walked over to the desk in the corner of the room and turned on the family computer.

"What are you doing?" asked Ryce.

"I'm going on-line," Ted said. "I'm going to cyber surf until I find a solution to this problem."

Mr. Newton, like most older people, had a deep mistrust of computers and could scarcely understand what the internet actually was. "Ted, you're not going to find anything there. It's just a gimmick . . ."

"Dad, when are you going to learn that the net knows everything?" Ted typed fast, logging on, then surfing to the world wide web. From there he went into a search mode. His sisters watched over his shoulder as the screen filled with data.

"See, Dad? Webcrawler has given me five pages of information on dog training," said Ted. "It's all here; you just have to know where to look."

"I'm not convinced," grumbled George Newton.

"You'll see . . ."

Ryce was busy reading the information on the screen. "Hey, this looks good. 'Get your dog in shape at Puppy Boot Camp—No Problem Too Big, No Dog Too Small.'"

Alice looked at George. "What do you think?"

"It's worth a shot, I guess," Mr. Newton replied.

"Should I E-mail them?" asked Ted eagerly.

"Why don't you just get the telephone number, honey?" said Mrs. Newton. "And we'll take it from there."

"Telephone," said Ted disgustedly. "How old-fashioned can you get? Next thing you know you're going to write them a letter and mail it with a stamp on it!"

Mr. Newton made the call that night and spoke to the owner of the Puppy Boot Camp, Colonel Jack Happer.

Happer was a bluff, gruff man with a deep voice and a commanding manner. Mr. Newton got the feeling that he would take no nonsense from any human or dog, but he wanted the man to be well forewarned.

"I have to tell you," said George Newton, "these dogs are rather . . . difficult cases. They've broken the spirit of one trainer already. She said—"

"You sent 'em to a woman? That was your first mistake. The woman ain't been born who can train a dog."

"Are you sure?"

"Course I'm sure, Newton. I got thirty years in the corps!"

"The . . . uh . . . corps? What corps?"

"The K-9 Corps!" Happer roared. "Where did you think I got this rank of colonel? Selling fried chicken?"

"No . . . I . . ."

"You bring them little doggies to me and I'll make sure they sit up and fly right. Those little pups will be so well trained you could lead 'em into combat."

"Sit and stay would be fine," said Mr. Newton.

"Yeah, that too."

The other Newtons were waiting anxiously to find out the results of the phone call to Puppy Boot Camp.

"Well," said George Newton, "it's all set."

"Tell us about it, Daddy," said Emily.

"Well, it's run by a man named Happer."

"Did he sound nice?" asked Royce.

"Well . . . He sounded military. He said he would make the puppies sit up and fly right."

"Is that good?" asked Ted.

"I think so . . . There's only one problem."

"What's that?" asked Mrs. Newton.

"It's a four-week course and it's up in the mountains." Mr. Newton paused. "I guess what I'm saying is that it really is a camp. The dogs would have to go away for a month."

Emily said what everyone was thinking. "A month? The puppies will be gone for a month? How will we ever explain it to Beethoven?!"

Chapter Five

THE DECISION TO SEND THE PUPPIES AWAY WAS A BITTERSWEET
one for the Newton children, but for Beethoven and Missy
it was a deeply disturbing event.

Emily, in particular, was anxious to make sure that the
two grown-up dogs knew exactly what was going on. She
draped her small arms across their burly shoulders and
hugged Beethoven and Missy close.

"I know you're sad because your babies are going away,"
she said. "But that's okay . . ."

The sorrow in Beethoven's eyes was obvious. Missy
whimpered faintly.

"But you have to understand that we would never let
anything bad happen to them. And before you know it,
they'll be back here, good as new. That's a promise,"

Beethoven and Missy licked Emily's hand and tried, for
her sake, not to look too upset about the departure of their
pups.

Bright and early the next morning, the entire Newton

family—five humans, six dogs—crowded into the family minivan and set off for Puppy Boot Camp. The drive was a long one—over fifty miles—and Mr. Newton had wanted to get going as soon as possible.

The puppies were as irrepressible as ever, but Beethoven and Missy were subdued and quiet. It seemed as if they never took their eyes off the puppies for the entire ride. Like most long car rides, this one was pretty boring to the kids— at least until the road started ascending into the mountains. Once they were up high, the road became narrow and curvy and from time to time they could catch a glimpse of breathtaking views of the valley below. The hillsides were heavily wooded with stands of tall pine trees, or else they were rocky and rugged and split with the rushing waters of mountainside streams.

The towns up in the mountains were small, remote, few and far between. "It seems like an awfully isolated place for a puppy farm," said Mrs. Newton. "How many people would drive this far to enroll their puppies in camp?"

"We're doing it," said Ted.

"We're desperate," said Ryce.

"I think it's good it's so remote," said Mr. Newton. "The puppies will stick to their studies."

Puppy Boot Camp was a collection of ramshackle old buildings at the very end of a very steep mountain road. There was a dilapidated main house and then a series of sheds and barns, all of them run-down and in need of a good paint job. There were two equally beat-up pickup trucks parked in front of the house.

"It doesn't look like they are doing very well," said Mrs. Newton. "I guess there aren't many people as desperate as we are."

"It makes sense," said Mr. Newton. "Why spend money on upkeep if the place is going to be destroyed by a pack of ravenous, rampaging puppies?"

As the car rolled to a halt in front of the house, a man emerged and stood on the top step, glaring down at the Newtons. He was a tall, broad-shouldered man, with a bullet-shaped head, his hair cut so short you could see his scalp. He was dressed from head to toe in military-style fatigues and had big black combat boots on his feet.

"That would be Colonel Happer," said George Newton.

"Good guess, dear," said Mrs. Newton.

Colonel Happer marched down the steps of the house and strode up to the van. "Who are you?" he barked.

Mr. Newton got out of the car. "George Newton, Colonel Happer. We spoke last night about having you train our puppies."

Happer nodded. "That's right. That's right. But I thought your ETA was oh-six-hundred."

"My what was when?"

"Your estimated time of arrive was six A.M."

"I don't think so, Colonel. We've come all the way from the city. We couldn't have gotten there by—"

"Cities! Got no use for 'em. Bad for dogs too."

Mr. Newton paled, suddenly afraid that after all this trouble Colonel Happer wouldn't take the dogs for training. "I'm sorry you don't like cities, Colonel, but—"

"So where are the recruits?"

"Recruits?"

"The dogs."

"Oh . . ." Mr. Newton tapped on the windshield of the car, motioning to his family.

The kids and the dogs tumbled out of the car. Released from confinement, the puppies raced around, barking loudly.

The puppies loved the smells of the countryside! It was so different from the neat suburbs. The dogs would run madly in one direction, smell a scent on the wind, come to a screeching halt and race in the other direction.

"You see our problem, Colonel," said Mrs. Newton.

"Indeed I do." He took a deep breath, his chest expanding like a pair of bellows. "Atten-*hut*!"

All the Newtons came to attention, but the puppies blithely ignored Colonel Happer, continuing to cavort in the dust and grass.

Colonel Happer's eyes blazed. "This is *insubordination*!"

"They do that a lot," Emily explained.

"Not around here they won't. There's *my way or hit the highway*." Colonel Happer took another deep breath. "*Puppies! Attenhut*!"

This time the puppies came to a screeching stop. Chubby looked quizzically at Colonel Happer, and ventured forward to sniff his boots. "Puppy! Halt!"

Chubby froze dead in her tracks.

"That's better," said Happer.

"It's nothing short of amazing," said Mr. Newton.

"Never met a dog I couldn't break," said the Colonel.

"We . . . we don't want them broken," said Ted. "Just trained."

Colonel Happer then did something very odd. He smiled. He had a lot of gold teeth and they glittered in the sun. "Don't you worry about that, young man. I'll train 'em till they can do everything but knit a sweater."

Mr. Newton and Colonel Happer went into the office to do the paperwork admitting the puppies to the Boot Camp. Mr. Newton signed form after form, hardly pausing to read the close-printed documents.

Colonel Happer looked over the forms and smiled. "Well, that's all. You're puppies are now in boot camp!"

The kids, Beethoven and Missy had their noses pressed to the glass of the rear window as the van drove away. The puppies watched, disbelieving, as the van bumped down the dirt road.

"Bye-bye," said Emily. She had tears in her eyes. "See you in four weeks."

Missy and Beethoven whimpered and put their paws up to the windows as if waving good-bye.

George Newton was pleased. "You know, I have a good feeling about this. Happer might be a disciplinarian, but that's what those puppies need."

"I was afraid I was going to drafted," said Mrs. Newton.

"He's harmless. And he'll get the job done."

"I suppose," said Mrs. Newton uneasily. "But you know what's strange about all this?"

George Newton nodded vigorously. "I know what's strange—what's strange is that we got the kids, Beethoven, Missy and the puppies to go along with it. That's the strangest thing of all."

"No," said Alice Newton. "That's not it . . ."

"What then?"

"Well, this is supposed to be the Puppy Boot Camp, right?"

"Right?"

"Then why weren't there any dogs there?"

Chapter Six

WHEN THE NEWTONS WERE FINALLY OUT OF SIGHT, Colonel Happer set about corralling the four puppies. Normally it wouldn't have been easy for one man to catch four small, active dogs, but Colonel Happer was wise to the ways of dogs—and he knew there was nothing they liked more than a little snack, particularly if it was a snack of freshly ground beef . . .

Happer went into the house and returned a few minutes later with two stainless steel bowls full of food. The puppies hadn't eaten since early that morning and they attacked the food avidly, the four of them crowding around, their noses deep in the bowls.

Colonel Happer watched the puppies guzzle and there was real affection in his eyes. He really had been in the K-9 corps and he did love dogs.

The Puppy Boot Camp wasn't doing very well, though, and he was worried about money. His pension from the army was all he had aside from the income from the Puppy

Boot Camp, and that was not much. To make matters worse, he had recently been forced to pay money to some clients whose dogs had mysteriously escaped from the farm.

The puppies finished their food and began licking their chops, trying to get every last scrap and taste of their delicious meal. They looked at Happer inquisitively, as if to say, "*Now* what will we do?"

Colonel Jack Happer knew exactly what they were going to do next—the puppies were going to go to sleep. He knew this not because he was an expert on dogs, but because he had mixed a very mild sedative in with the puppy chow. He knew the dogs would get distraught when they were left alone, and he didn't want them to be.

Sure enough the puppies felt themselves getting sleepy and sluggish, their eyes heavy. One by one, they put their little heads down and fell asleep . . .

Happer picked up two dogs in each arm and walked across the front yard of the old house to a decrepit old shed. He put the dogs down in a bed of torn-up newspaper and left them there, locking the door behind him.

Colonel Jack Happer did not run Puppy Boot Camp by himself. He had an assistant who went by the name of Arthur Smith. That wasn't his real name, of course: "Arthur" wouldn't want anyone to know who he really was.

He was, in fact, an old hand at dog-napping—his name was Walter Varnick. Once upon a time he had been known as Dr. Varnick, a veterinarian who had once owned a shady outfit called Dandy Pup Pet Supply, and also once upon a time treated Beethoven!

Dr. Varnick, along with his evil assistants, Vernon and Harvey, had dog-napped dogs for illegal medical experiments and, because of Beethoven, had gone to jail for it.

Unfortunately, you don't go to prison for long if your crime is cruelty to animals, and Varnick had been released just the month before. He could no longer practice as a veterinarian, but he could still work with animals. He had gotten his job with Colonel Happer and immediately realized that there was more money to be made from the Puppy Boot Camp than from just training naughty dogs.

Twice in the last six months, dogs had come in for training that Varnick knew were worth a lot of money. In the dead of night, after Colonel Happer had gone to bed, Varnick would sneak the puppies out of the barns and drive down to the valley, where he sold the animals to a pet shop owner he knew from the old days. The pet shop owner didn't ask any questions about the dogs and, even better, he always paid cash. It was up to the Colonel to explain to the upset owners that their beloved dogs had escaped and to make amends by paying compensation.

Colonel Happer found Varnick in the office when he returned from locking up the puppies. Varnick was slumped in a chair, drinking a cup of coffee and reading an out-of-date copy of *Dog World*.

He scarcely looked up when the Colonel came in. Although Happer was supposed to be the boss and owner of Puppy Boot Camp, Varnick treated him as if he were nothing more than a lowly employee.

"What did you get?" Varnick asked.

"Four purebred Saint Bernard pups," said Happer. "Cute little guys too. They're pretty rambunctious but you have to expect that."

"Saint Bernards," said Varnick, sitting up in his chair. "I don't like Saint Bernards. I've had a lot of trouble with Saint Bernards."

"Really," said Happer. "I've always found them pretty easy to work with. What was your trouble with them?"

"I don't want to talk about it," said Varnick gruffly. The last thing he wanted to do was relive his disastrous encounter with Beethoven. If it hadn't been for that Saint Bernard, he would still be a vet—and he would never have gone to jail.

"Well," said Happer, "you better be ready bright and early tomorrow. I promised to have those dogs in tip-top shape when the owners come back in a month."

"No hurry," said Varnick, returning to his magazine.

"Smith!" yelled the Colonel. "I won't stand for slackers in my outfit. Understand?"

Varnick/Smith sighed heavily and groaned. But there weren't a lot of places he could find work, so he had to keep his job or go hungry.

"Four Saint Bernards, huh, Colonel?" he said.

"That's right. We start putting them through their paces first thing in the morning. Understand?"

"Yeah . . . I understand." Slowly Varnick got to his feet. "I'll go take a look at 'em right now."

"Good man. I like a soldier to show a little initiative."

"Yeah. Right."

Varnick made his way to the barn. Despite his dislike of Saint Bernards, he knew that a lot of stupid, misguided people liked them. And he knew that they would pay good money for the right pup. He figured he could live with his dislike of Saint Bernards long enough to make a little more money . . .

The Newtons were silent on the way home. The kids were missing the puppies already, as were Missy and Beethoven. Alice Newton was alone with her worries about the Puppy

Boot Camp—she felt uneasy about the place. It seemed so empty and desolate. Colonel Happer was certainly an eccentric, but he seemed harmless enough. Still there was something about the place that bothered her.

George Newton, on the other hand, was feeling satisfied, quietly savoring his triumph. He had managed to get the puppies out of his hair for four whole weeks. And at the end of that time, when they were perfectly trained, maybe—just maybe—he'd be able to convince the kids to let him sell the dogs. That would mean four thousand dollars . . . And he felt he deserved it after all he had been through.

From the backseat Emily called out to her father. "Daddy, I miss the puppies . . . I miss the puppies a lot."

George Newton sighed. The puppies, always the puppies . . . "I know, honey, but they'll be back soon enough. And they'll be better than before."

"But I'm afraid they're afraid up there without us."

"That's just plain silly, Emily," said Mrs. Newton soothingly. "They're going to have a great time up in the mountains. Saint Bernards are mountain dogs, you know. This is chance for the puppies to get to know their natural environment."

"They are?" said Emily. "Maybe we should move to the mountains to make the puppies happier."

"Where would Daddy work?" Ted asked.

"He could stay in the town and come home on weekends," said Emily, who appeared to have it all figured out already.

"Thanks a lot," said George Newton.

"Well, you wouldn't be around the puppies all the time," Emily countered. "You'd like that, wouldn't you?"

Of course, nothing would have delighted Mr. Newton

more, but he knew that he couldn't say that to his daughter. "No, that's not true at all, honey."

"It isn't?"

"Of course not."

"You like puppies?"

"You know I do."

"Can we get some more?"

"Yeah, George," said Mrs. Newton dryly. "Can we?"

"I don't think we have to do that, honey," said Mr. Newton. "But in the meantime I'll bet the puppies are really enjoying themselves . . ."

Chapter Seven

MOE WAS THE FIRST PUPPY TO WAKE UP THAT NIGHT. ONE moment he was dreaming a wonderful dream about mounds and mounds of delicious plastic, and the next thing he knew he was wide awake in a strange, dark room, with no idea where he was. He jumped to his feet and sniffed the air, searching the darkness for a smell he recognized. He was delighted and relieved to find that his brothers and sisters were nearby, but he could find no trace of Missy and Beethoven. Neither was there the scent of the Newtons. There were many strange, unfamiliar odors too and they scared him. The little puppy stood there, trembling in the dark. Soon he began to whimper.

The fretful fussing woke the other puppies. They too wondered where they were—and where were the people they loved? Soon all four were huddling together, pooling their worry and fear and deriving some measure of relief from the warmth of one another.

Slowly, they began to remember what had happened that

day: the long ride in the van, the sudden appearance of the tall, noisy man. And, most distressing of all, watching the van drive down the road, over the hill and out of sight.

"Have they left us forever?" Chubby wondered.

"Would they? Could they?" wondered Dolly.

"They wouldn't!" Tchaikovsky insisted. "They would never do that! You've seen how they love us!"

"We're being punished," Moe declared firmly. "That's it! They'll keep us in here one night and then all will be forgiven."

Whatever the reason, the puppies were scared—more scared than they had ever been before in their short lives.

"What shall we do?" asked Dolly.

"Stay put," said Moe. "And we stay calm. We stay put, and come the morning this whole thing will be over."

"Are you sure?" asked Tchaikovsky.

"Yes!" said Moe stoutly. He could not believe that Missy and Beethoven as well as the Newtons would have abandoned them to the terrible place.

"But this isn't our house," said Dolly. "We saw them driving away. We're never going to see them again." That said, Dolly, who tended to be an alarmist, started to wail piteously, a howl immediately taken up by Tchaikovsky.

"Stop it!" Moe insisted. "Stop that right now!"

"I caaaaan't!" Dolly lamented. "It's hard to stop once you get started, you know. I'm so sorry . . ."

"You're upsetting everyone!" said Chubby. There was nothing that made a dog want to howl more than hearing another dog howl. It was all Chubby could do to resist the temptation to join in.

"Tchaikovsky! Stop moaning!"

"I can't help it either!" Tchaikovsky wailed. "I know it's useless, but somehow it makes me feel better!"

As Chubby listened to her brothers and sisters, she could feel her resolve weakening. Then, finally, she succumbed to the temptation and opened her mouth wide and let out a louder howl than anyone!

Moe looked at the other pups with disgust. But then decided if he couldn't beat them, he might as well join in. Suddenly, he let out a wail that almost drowned out the other three puppies combined.

The four puppies cried and howled, louder and louder, sending their impassioned cries out into the night, trying to send their message out to Missy and Beethoven, telling them that they were scared, they were hungry and they wanted to be rescued. They had no idea, of course, that Beethoven and Missy were nowhere near to them.

But some people could hear them . . .

As the puppies howled, the door of the barn was thrown open and a bright shaft of light stabbed into the room. The puppies were so startled and scared that they stopped howling and the fur on their backs stood up straight.

"What's all this noise?" said a voice. The bright light from the flashlight was so dazzling that the puppies could not see the man who spoke to them. But they understood the tone and they could tell that this man was no friend.

Varnick shone the light around the room, as if searching for an interloper. "Anyone get in here? No? Well, you darn pups better pipe down. Understand?"

The four little dogs huddled together even more closely and put their heads down as if they thought that if they couldn't see him, Varnick would just disappear.

But he didn't. Instead, he turned the flashlight on his face and scowled at the puppies. "Now, listen up. I don't like

Saint Bernards," he said. "In fact, I don't like dogs all that much. So I'm gonna make it my business to have you off the property and into a pet store faster than lightning. That old fool up in the house can't save you and neither can your owners. In the meantime, you stay outta my way and you won't get hurt. Understand? Good!" With that, Varnick snapped off the light and slammed the door. A second later they heard the lock snap shut.

Now the puppies were really scared!

"Did . . . did he say . . . pet shop?" asked Dolly, on the verge of tears.

"Yes, he did," Moe confirmed.

"That's bad," said Tchaikovsky.

"Really bad," said Chubby.

Among Beethoven's children there were no more terrifying words than "pet shop." All of the puppies had heard their father's terrifying stories of his days in a pet shop back when he was a little puppy himself. They had also heard the story of Beethoven's misadventures with the evil Dr. Varnick. Of course, not one of the puppies had been alive then and they had no way of knowing that they had fallen into the clutches of the very same evil man who had threatened their father all those years ago.

"I can't believe that they would let this happen to us," said Dolly. "It's really, really unfair."

"Why? Why? That's what I can't understand," put in Chubby. "We were never anything but perfect at home, were we?"

"I thought we were wonderful."

"The children always liked us," said Tchaikovsky. "You don't suppose it could have had anything to do with us chewing up stuff?"

The other three puppies looked perplexed. "Naawwww," said Chubby, finally.

"I'll tell you one thing I know for sure," said Moe.

"What?" asked Dolly.

"We have to get out of here—for sure."

Chapter Eight

THE PHONE STARTED RINGING IN THE OFFICE OF PUPPY BOOT Camp just after midnight, and it rang and rang, the loud bell trilling at least thirty times before Colonel Happer woke up. He swept aside the sheets and blankets and strode out of his bedroom, into the hallway beyond.

"Smith!" the Colonel bellowed. "Front and center—at the double!"

There was no answer from Varnick's room except for some loud, deep, throaty snores. All the while the phone continued to ring and ring.

The Colonel growled and thundered down the corridor and threw open the door. "Smith! Wake up!"

Colonel Happer made so much noise that Varnick sat straight up in bed. "I didn't do it! I was never anywhere near the place, Officer!"

"*What?*"

"Oh," said Varnick bitterly. "It's you." He fumbled for his thick glasses and put them on. "What do you want?"

"The land line is ringing. Get your skinny butt downstairs and answer it!"

Varnick squinted at Colonel Happer as if he had suddenly grown two heads. "The land line? What's a land line?" He also noticed that Colonel Happer had a row of medals pinned on the chest of his pajamas.

"The telephone. Go answer it."

Varnick snuggled down in bed. "You're already up," he said. "Why don't you go down and answer the land line?"

"Because I'm the officer in charge, mister," Colonel Happer bellowed. "And if the service taught me anything, I learned that there is room for only one top kick in any outfit! Now, move it!"

Grumbling, Varnick crawled out of his warm and comfy bed. "You always wear medals on your pajamas?"

"If you'd won 'em, you'd wear 'em too, mister!"

Cursing and muttering under his breath, Varnick made his way down to the office, where the phone continued to ring stridently. He snatched up the receiver as if he were about to take a bite out of it.

"What? What? Who is that? Calling at this time of the night—you oughtta be ashamed of yourself. People sleeping here, ya know!"

A very small voice said, "Please may I speak to Chubby, Dolly, Tchaikovsky and Moe, please?"

Varnick actually stared at the phone, as if the machine had suddenly gone crazy and was making crank calls all on its own. "What?" he demanded angrily.

"I said, please may I talk to Chubby, Dolly, Tchaikovsky and Moe please. And could you hurry up . . ."

"What are you talking about?" yelled Varnick. "Who is that?"

"My name is Emily Newton and I would please like to talk to my puppies Dolly, Chubby, Tchaikovsky and Moe please." Back in the Newtons' house Emily glanced toward the stairs, sure that she was going to hear her father or mother coming down at any moment.

Emily had been lying in bed for hours, tormented by her longing for her pets. Finally, sometime after midnight, unable to stand it anymore, she had stolen downstairs and got on the phone in the kitchen.

"Please hurry," she urged Varnick. "I don't have a lot of time."

"What? Are you nuts! You want to talk to your dogs?"

"Yes, please. I miss them. They're just little Saint Bernard puppies and they've never been away from Missy and Beethoven before. I know they're probably scared and I wanted them to know that we're thinking about them and that they'll be coming home soon." Emily paused for breath. "So if you could put them on . . . I guess I'd like to talk to Tchaikovsky first, if that's okay. And if they're sleeping, you can wake them up. I'm sure they won't mind."

Varnick couldn't quite believe his ears. "Listen, I don't know who you are, but I know that you better get—"

"I'm Emily Newton," Emily repeated.

Varnick paused. In the back of his mind a bell began to ring softly, then, as his brain connected all the dots, the bell began to ring louder. "Little girl . . . what did you say your name was?"

"Emily Newton."

"And what did you say your dog's name was?"

"Chubby, Tchaikovsky, Dolly and—"

"No, no." Varnick interrupted. "The big dog. The daddy dog."

"His name is Beethoven," said Emily proudly. "And the mommy dog's name is Missy."

"I don't care about her," Varnick snapped. "Beethoven, huh? That's a very nice name for a dog . . ."

"He's a very nice dog," said Emily.

"I'll bet he is," said Varnick with a little snarl in his voice. He could not believe it! The very people who had ruined him, his business, had put him in jail and stripped him of his license to practice as a vet—they were now in his power. He had their puppies and he was going to make them pay for all the harm they had done him.

"Listen, little girl," said Varnick, attempting to inject some sweetness into his voice (it wasn't easy), "I'm afraid your little doggies are sound asleep and I would hate to disturb their rest right now."

"I'm sure they wouldn't mind," Emily insisted. "Sometimes they wake me up in the night and I don't mind."

Varnick did his best to control his temper. "I think you better hang up and go to sleep now, Emily."

"But I *have* to speak to them," Emily protested. "I *have* to know that they are all right and that they understand that they'll be coming home."

"Well, you can't," said Varnick. "And that's final!"

"Oh, no!" Emily said suddenly. "Daddy!"

An adult voice replaced Emily's on the phone. "This is George Newton. Who is this please?"

"Uh, this is—" For a moment Varnick had trouble thinking of the name he had adopted when he got out of prison. "This is Jones . . . I mean Smith. Your little girl called here to the Puppy Boot Camp to talk to her puppies." Varnick did his best to chuckle. "Cute. Real cute. Ha-ha . . ."

Varnick heard Newton exhale heavily, as if in disappointment. "I apologize, Mr. Smith," he said. "It won't happen again."

"No trouble, no harm done, Mr. Newton. Good night." Varnick hung up the phone and clapped his hands happily. "Now, that was a phone call worth getting up in the middle of the night for."

He went back upstairs. The Colonel was waiting for him with his arms folded across his barrel chest. "What was that all about?"

"Uh . . . wrong number, Colonel."

"Huh. Took you long enough."

"It was a *really* wrong number."

"Well," the Colonel ordered. "Get back in your rack. Reveille is at oh-six-thirty sharp. Understand?"

"Yessir! Colonel sir!"

"Good," said Happer. "That's better."

Varnick went back to bed, but he was too excited to sleep. There was only one thing he liked better than money— revenge! And now he would have it!

Chapter Nine

AS THE FIRST RAYS OF THE MORNING SUN CREPT INTO THE old barn, the puppies began to wake from their fitful, uneasy sleep. Chubby, Tchaikovsky, Dolly and Moe woke and immediately felt themselves plunged into despair. Sleep, however restless, had been an escape from their horrible predicament. When they awoke, they realized that they had not found themselves trapped in a terrible nightmare—this was for real.

"Oh, no," Dolly whimpered. She was looking around the room and blinking sadly. "This is terrible . . ."

"We have to escape," said Moe.

"But how?" asked Tchaikovsky.

Moe sniffed the floor. "This is nothing but dirt. We could tunnel our way out."

"That would take forever!" Dolly wailed.

"Not if we all work together," said Tchaikovsky.

"But it will still take forever!" said Dolly sorrowfully.

Suddenly Chubby sat up and sniffed the air avidly. "Hey!" she barked. "Do you all smell what I smell?"

"What?" asked Moe.

"Food!"

The other three puppies stuck their noses in the air and sniffed. Sure enough, they could smell the sweet aroma of food wafting into the barn on the edge of a morning breeze.

"I hope that food is headed our way," said Chubby, licking her chops hungrily. "I'm starving!"

"There are more important things right now than food," said Moe sternly. "We have to get out of here."

"Absolutely," said Chubby. "We'll get out of here as soon as breakfast is over. Is that okay?"

"No," said Moe. "I think we should just rush out the door the moment it's opened. They won't be expecting that. All we have to do is get through that door and outside. Then we make a run for the forest."

"You . . . you mean just run away?" Dolly asked uncertainly. "Won't that be sort of dangerous?"

"Not as dangerous as staying here," said Tchaikovsky.

"That's right," Moe agreed. "You heard what that man said last night. He's going to get rid of us. That means we'll be split up. And that means we'll never see each other again. Or Mom or Dad. Or the Newtons."

"Oh, no," whimpered Dolly. That was the worst thing she had ever heard. "Are you *sure* they aren't coming back for us?"

"No," said Moe. "I'm not sure . . . But I don't want to take the chance either. I say we run."

"Me too," said Tchaikovsky.

Dolly and Chubby looked at each other uncertainly.

"I suppose we better go too," said Dolly.

"Without getting anything to eat?" Chubby asked sadly. "Isn't that a little . . . unwise? I mean, shouldn't we keep up our strength before we make a run for it?"

"No," said Moe firmly. "Getting out is the important thing. We can worry about food when we've escaped."

Just then the door swung open and Varnick stood there with two big bowls of kibble in his hands. "Here you go, you miserable little—"

"Now!" Moe barked. "Let's go!" Suddenly the four puppies bounded for the door, yipping and yapping as they raced between Varnick's legs.

"What the—!" Varnick danced and dodged, trying to avoid the puppies under his feet. Then he toppled over, scattering kibble everywhere.

The puppies were out in the fresh air now, Moe leading the charge for the woods that encircled the property. Colonel Happer was just coming out of the house as the puppies made their bid for freedom. He knew instantly what was going on.

"Puppies!" he bellowed. "Halt!"

But the puppies did not stop, running for the woods as fast as their little legs would carry them.

"*Halt!*" Happer shouted at the top of his lungs. "*That's an order!*" He turned around and yelled at Varnick, who was still sprawled on the ground. "Smith! Get your butt in gear and get after them!"

When Moe reached the beginning of the woods, he stopped and looked back. There was Tchaikovsky. There was Dolly . . . But where was Chubby?

Suddenly, Moe saw her. "Oh no!" he cried.

Chubby had been unable to resist the temptation of a great big breakfast—the little dog was back at the barn door greedily gobbling up the kibble that had spilled all over the ground in front of the barn.

"Chubby! Chubby!" Moe yelled. "Run! Run before they catch you!" Chubby heard Moe's impassioned barking and she looked up from her breakfast. Seeing her brothers and sisters already in the forest seemed to shock her out of her hunger. They were leaving and she was so far behind!

All of a sudden, she started to run. But it was too late—Varnick swooped down behind her and grabbed her. Chubby wriggled and squirmed, but she couldn't break free of Varnick's strong arms.

"Gotcha!" Varnick yelled. "Thought you could get away from me, huh? Well, you're nothin' but a dumb animal, don't you forget that!"

In the forest, the remaining three puppies were panic-stricken. They didn't know what to do next.

"Oh, this is terrible!" Dolly wailed. "What are we going to do!"

"We can't leave without Chubby," said Tchaikovsky.

They watched as Varnick threw Chubby back into the barn and slammed the door, locking it firmly. Then he and the Colonel started toward the woods.

"They're coming to look for us," said Tchaikovsky urgently. "Moe! Tell us what to do! Quick!"

"There's only one thing we can do," said Moe sadly. "We can't leave Chubby behind, so we're going to have to go back."

Chapter Ten

COLONEL HAPPER WAS OF THE OPINION THAT DOGS SHOULD not be punished if they didn't know they had done wrong. Neither he nor Varnick imagined that the puppies were making an attempt to escape—rather, the little dogs were just showing a burst high spirits after being cooped up in the barn all night. Of course, Colonel Happer didn't know that Varnick had already told the pups just what was in store for them in the very near future.

The Colonel had Varnick put choke collars and leashes on all four dogs, then he lined them up in front of the house.

The Colonel walked back and forth in front of the puppies. The dogs watched him, hoping to hear something encouraging in his voice. They knew Varnick to be evil but they weren't sure about the Colonel—they could only hope.

"You have been sent here for training," the Colonel growled. "You will find that this training is rigorous in the extreme, but when it is completed, you will be some of the finest trained dogs in this man's army!"

"What's an army?" Tchaikovsky asked.

Moe just shrugged his shoulders. "Dunno."

Colonel Happer continued. "Mr. Smith here, will be taking care of you full-time, while I shall be overseeing the entire training program."

"Oh, I don't like the sound of that," said Chubby morosely.

"And now," said Colonel Happer, "your training will begin forthwith. When your owners return for you in four weeks time, I want you to be proficient in all forms of canine discipline. Make me proud, pups!"

"Did you hear that?" said Dolly, sounding hopeful for the first time in a long, long time. "He said our owners are returning!"

"That's right," yapped Tchaikovsky. "We're saved!"

"No, we're not," said Moe wearily. "The other man said he was going to steal us and sell us before the Newtons come back."

"Oh . . . ," said Dolly sadly, her hope evaporating as quickly as it had sprung to life. "That's right . . ."

"All right, puppies," Varnick yelled, "let's move it!" He grabbed all four leashes and walked them to a large concrete slab encircled by a tall chain-link cyclone fence. He unlocked the door and tethered three of the dogs to a post, but kept Tchaikovsky with him. The Colonel stood in the middle of the concrete court and faced Varnick and the dog.

"*Sit!*" ordered the Colonel in his best parade-ground voice. Tchaikovsky blinked and looked at the Colonel as if the man had suddenly taken leave of his senses.

"Puppy! The order is *sit*!"

The moment the Colonel shouted "sit," Varnick grasped Tchaikovsky's hindquarters and firmly pushed them down, making him sit. The trouble was, Tchaikovsky did not want to sit, so the instant his butt touched the ground it popped right back up as if it were mounted on steel springs.

"No, no, no," grumbled the Colonel. "That's not good. Smith! Let's do it again till we get it right."

"I've never been so bored in my life," Varnick grumbled under his breath. "I've got to get out of here before I go completely nuts."

"Smith! What are you mumbling over there, mister?" the Colonel yelled.

"I said 'no ifs, ands or buts,' sir!" Then Varnick lowered his voice to a whisper and said, "You lunatic old moron."

"*Sit!*" the Colonel bellowed. Tchaikovsky continued to look at the man quizzically. Varnick pushed his hindquarters down and immediately they popped right back up again.

This rather pointless game went on for some time, until Tchaikovsky got tired of standing and did sit down—and it just happened to coincide with one of the Colonel's commands that he do just that!

"Good dog!" shouted the Colonel. "That's a very good dog!" Happer was beaming at Tchaikovsky proudly. "Smith," the Colonel ordered, "tell the doggy he did good."

"Good dog," said Varnick through clenched teeth.

"Say it like you mean it Smith!"

"Goooooooood doggy," said Varnick. "Goood, goood, goooood doggy. That's a good little doggy . . ."

Dolly, Chubby and Moe looked puzzled, amazed at all the attention and praise being lavished on their brother.

"What's the big deal?" Chubby asked. "All he did was sit down."

"I know," said Moe. "Humans, they make no sense . . . I don't think I'll ever figure them out."

"*Next!*" ordered Colonel Happer.

Varnick brought Tchaikovsky back to the group, tethered him and took Dolly out on the court.

"*Sit!*" the Colonel yelled.

Dolly figured that if Tchaikovsky got all that praise for sitting, she could get even more for doing something extra. So she sat down, then rolled over and stuck her legs in the air.

"Hoo boy," said Varnick. "This is hopeless."

The Colonel spent the rest of the morning yelling "sit" at the dogs, a game that got sort of tiresome after a while. Sometimes one of the dogs would sit, but most of the time they just stood around wondering what on earth was going on.

Finally, the Colonel looked at the big watch on his wrist and shouted, "Okay! That will be enough for the morning. There will now follow a twenty-five-minute break for chow . . . Smith!"

"Now what?" Varnick muttered.

"*Smith!*"

"Yessir, Colonel sir!"

"I leave you in charge. Carry on!" With that, the Colonel marched off the court.

Varnick grabbed the four leashes and pulled the dogs toward the gate. "Come on, you mutts. I got better things to do with my break than mess with you." He yawned heavily. "I didn't get a lot of sleep last night because of that darn fool little girl calling up wanting to talk to her puppies! Can you believe it!"

"Emily," said Moe. "That must have been Emily!"

"She misses us," said Dolly. "We have to get home to her!"

"Just as soon as we've had lunch," said Chubby. "Right?"

Chapter Eleven

ALL OF THE PUPPIES—NOT JUST CHUBBY—WERE GRATEFUL for the bowls of food and water that Varnick set out for them. Only Chubby had had anything to eat since the night before, and they devoured the food and slurped up the water in a hurry.

Varnick paid no attention to them as he sprawled on the grass ten or fifteen yards away. He ate a sandwich, drank a soda, took a quick look at his watch and glanced over at the puppies, scowling at them.

"The Colonel's going to be out in fifteen minutes," he said. "I'm going to take a little nap for myself. You all stay right where you are, you understand me, you miserable little balls of fluff?"

Moe did his best to look obedient. In order to lull the man into trusting him, he put his head down on his paws and closed his eyes as if he were to follow Varnick's example and get a little shut-eye.

Varnick closed his eyes as well and a few moments later he was snoring gently, his mouth open.

Moe looked at the sleeping man and then over at his brother and sister. He could not believe the amazing stroke of luck they had just been handed. "This is actually a little easier than I thought it was going to be."

Very quietly, the four puppies got to their feet and stole away, running silent for the woods and freedom . . .

Varnick was having a wonderful dream. He was somewhere warm and pleasant and he knew he had a lot of money and somehow he had managed to get rid of all the puppies in only a matter of minutes. Somewhere in the back of his mind he could hear an angry voice, someone calling for Smith, but that didn't bother him, his name wasn't—

"*Smith!*"

The Colonel was standing over Varnick, his face red and contorted, the veins in his neck standing out like thick cables. "*Smith! What in the sam hill did you do with the puppies!?*"

Varnick jumped to his feet and gaped at where the puppies had been, amazed that they were gone. "I . . . I . . . They . . . But . . . Ah . . ."

"*You were sleeping on duty, mister, and in the service we used to court-martial men for that, mister!*"

"They have to be around here some someplace, Colonel."

"Look around you, Smith! Wake and smell the decaf, mister! You see any puppies around here?"

Varnick looked around quickly and saw that, indeed, there was no sign of the four little dogs.

"Well, if they got into the woods, they won't get far," said Varnick. "They're just dumb little puppies."

"Dumb, huh?" the Colonel growled. "Well, those dumb little puppies sure managed to outsmart you, mister!"

*   *   *

The puppies ran as fast as they could for as long as they could, scampering deeper and deeper into the woods. The trouble was they kept on snagging their leashes on tree stumps and branches, tumbling over as the leather cords caught and tightened, almost strangling each one of them.

Gradually, they slowed, their hearts pounding in their chests, their lungs aching from the effort of running so fast. They flopped down on the carpet of the soft pine needles on the ground, a big pile of puppy under the branches of a tall pine tree. All of the trees were close together and it was cool and dark in the forest—the only sound was the panting of the four dogs.

"Do you think they're following us? I hope not," Dolly asked. She raised her head and looked back the way they came. "I don't see anyone."

Tchaikovsky cocked an ear. "I don't hear anyone."

"And I don't smell anyone," said Chubby, sampling the light breeze that wafted through the trees.

"We have to keep moving," said Moe. "Maybe they aren't nearby now, but I'm sure they will be chasing us."

"We can't keep going," said Chubby, "not with these leashes around our necks. I almost throttled myself."

"Me too," said Tchaikovsky.

"The leashes have to go," said Dolly. "I don't think I can run much farther with this thing on."

Moe swiveled his head in an attempt to look at the thick steel swivel lock that clipped the leash to his collar. "What are we going to do?" he said. "I don't know how these things work."

"Well," Chubby said. "You know, I do have a certain taste for leather . . . I could chew them off . . ."

"Of course," said Moe. "That's exactly what we'll do!"

Chubby began chewing on the leash attached to Dolly's collar and Moe started on Tchaikovsky's. The leather was stiff and tough, but the puppies had needle-sharp teeth and were, as we well know, very enthusiastic chewers. They gnawed and chomped, eating away at the leather until it was in tatters.

As soon as the leads on Dolly and Tchaikovsky had been chewed away, they took their turn chomping at the leashes on Moe and Chubby. Soon all four were free, and they felt pretty good about that. Not only were they free of their leashes, they had also had themselves a really good chew and that always made them feel better.

The four little puppies sat for a moment, wondering what to do next. It was Dolly—who had an uncanny ability to see the unpleasant side of anything—who spoke next.

"Do you realize," she said in a small voice, "that this is the first time we have ever, ever, in our whole lives, been alone?"

The four puppies shivered as they realized that Dolly spoke the truth. Suddenly, the deep dark forest did not seem such a pleasant place to be.

Chapter Twelve

COLONEL HAPPER WAS A STRONG MAN, AN OLD SOLDIER NOT much given to self-pity, despondency or despair, but he was beginning to think that the Puppy Boot Camp was doomed. Now, for the third time since he had opened the establishment, a pack of puppies had disappeared. In addition, it meant that the insurance premiums that he paid would skyrocket, and the extra expense might be the last straw, the thing that just might put him out of business once and for all.

But there was something worse than that. Colonel Happer, as a soldier, had a strong sense of duty and integrity. Honor required that he tell the Newtons immediately what had happened. And that meant he had to confront angry adults and, worse, crying, sorrowful children.

With a heavy heart the Colonel dialed the Newtons' telephone number, steeling himself for an angry tirade from George Newton.

But it was even worse than that. Colonel Happer winced

when he heard the voice of a small girl answering the phone.

The Colonel cleared his throat. "Hello," he said, trying not to sound like a six-foot-six, two-hundred-and-fifty-pound ex-military man. "Can I please speak to your daddy, little girl?"

"He's not here," said Emily.

"Oh," said Happer, at a loss for words for a moment. "Can I please talk to your mommy, then?"

"She's not here either," said Emily.

"Is there someone there I can talk to, by any chance?" the Colonel said, unhappy at this turn of events.

"You can talk to me," said Emily promptly. "How about that?"

"Er, um, ahem . . ." The Colonel cleared his throat roughly. "Yes, um, I see that."

Colonel Happer had no children of his own and he was unused to them and that made him uncomfortable. He was not aware of the irony of the fact that this huge, gruff, old soldier—a man who had faced enemies in combat without flinching—had been reduced to a stammering, sweating, tongue-tied coward by a little girl still in grade school.

"Hello?" said Emily. "Are you still there?"

Suddenly, Colonel Happer lost his nerve. "Thank you, I'll call back later," he said quickly and slammed down the phone. "Hoo boy. That was terrible." He wiped the sweat from his brow and sighed heavily. Then he caught sight of Varnick lurking outside the office.

"You finished with the phone, Colonel? 'Cause I gotta make a call. It's really urgent."

The Colonel was glad to replace terror with anger. "*You!*" he roared. "You are the cause of this calamity! I should have known you were trouble the first moment I set eyes on you!"

Varnick just shrugged. "Yeah . . . well . . . Sorry about that. How about letting me use the phone?"

"No!" He snatched up the phone and dialed the Newtons' number again. This time Mr. Newton answered the call—to Colonel Happer's immense relief. The two men spoke for a few minutes and agreed that Happer and his assistant, "Smith," would institute a search for the puppies immediately.

"But," said Mr. Newton, "only if it isn't too much trouble. I mean, if you're busy, don't bother."

"I insist," said Colonel Happer stoutly. "It is my duty as a soldier to return your pups to you." The Colonel hung up, feeling a lot better.

"How did he take it?" asked Varnick.

"You know . . . ," said Happer, "not bad. Not bad at all. He's a cool one, that George Newton. Course I used to see guys like that in the service all the time. Cool under fire, always keeps his wits. Never gets upset. It's like they have ice water in their veins and steel in their bones."

Varnick rolled his eyes. "Oh, yeah, that's George Newton all right."

"How do you know?" asked Happer. "You know him?"

"Uh . . . No . . . I just . . . huh—hey! Can I use that phone now?"

Chapter Thirteen

GEORGE NEWTON'S HEART BEAT A LITTLE FASTER AFTER HE hung up with Colonel Happer. While he didn't want to see any harm befall the puppies, he was glad to hear that there was a chance that they might be out of his hair once and for all. What he really hoped was that some nice people would find the puppies and give them good homes. End of problem . . . Except . . . How would he break it to his family? They would not see the situation as favorably as he did.

"Who was on the phone, dear?" Mrs. Newton asked when he returned to the dining table.

"Oh . . . ," said Mr. Newton. "It was only"—he took an enormous bite of his dinner—"Ernal apper," he said, his mouth filled with food.

"Who?" asked Alice Newton.

Mr. Newton swallowed. "What do you mean? I thought I just told you who was on the phone."

Mrs. Newton's eyes narrowed and she peered at her

husband. She knew him too well—far too well for him to try and put something over on her. Mr. Newton went back to his dinner as if nothing were going on at all.

"George, tell me again."

But by this time, Mr. Newton's mouth was full again. "*Ernal Apper.*"

"George," said Mrs. Newton sternly. "What are you playing at? And do not talk with your mouth full, you're setting a bad example."

"Now we're all going to want to do it," said Ted.

"Who was on the phone? Tell me clearly this time."

"Colonel Happer," said George Newton.

"Colonel Happer!" said Emily. "How are the puppies? Are they okay? Did something happen to them?"

"Now, I want everyone to stay calm . . . ," said Mr. Newton. Which were the exact words that would insure that everyone got upset.

"Daddy!" Emily shrieked. "What happened!"

"George!"

"Dad, tell us," Ryce demanded.

"Yeah," insisted Ted.

"It seems that the puppies have . . . escaped from Puppy Boot Camp," said Mr. Newton reluctantly.

"Oh, no!" Emily wailed.

"How did that happen?" Mrs. Newton demanded.

"Yeah!"

"Tell us, Daddy."

"Well, it seems that the man who was supposed to be watching them fell asleep and the puppies just walked off the property. Now, I don't want anyone to worry, because Colonel Happer tells me he's going to find them and return them to us, good as new." In his mind, Mr. Newton was crossing his fingers, praying that what he said was not, in fact, true.

"They're out in the forest?" moaned Emily. "All by themselves." Tears started into her eyes as she thought about how scared the puppies must be.

"They must be terrified," said Ted.

"Poor things," said Ryce. She was feeling a little teary herself.

"Please, I asked you all to remain calm," said Mr. Newton testily.

"We have to go find them," said Ted.

"Definitely," said Emily. "Daddy, go start the car."

But Mr. Newton shook his head. "We're not going up into the mountains to look for the dogs. Colonel Happer assures me that everything will be all right. We'll just have to take his word for it."

"That's not good enough," said Ted. "We have to go and rescue them, Dad."

"Out of the question," said Mr. Newton firmly.

"Mommy!" pleaded Emily. "Tell Dad that we have to go and rescue the puppies. Right now!"

"I have to agree with your father," said Alice Newton. "I think we should leave this matter up to the Colonel and his assistant."

"His assistant?" said Ryce angrily. "It was his fault that the puppies escaped in the first place!"

"Yeah," said Ted. "We don't know who he is. We didn't even meet him. He could be anyone."

"I spoke to him," said Emily. "Daddy spoke to him too."

Everybody stopped and stared at her.

"You spoke to him?" said Ryce. "How? When?"

"Emily got up in the night and called the Puppy Boot Camp," Mr. Newton explained. "I caught her."

"And let me tell you, that assistant or whatever he was was not a nice man. I'm sure he's a bad man."

"Honey, you can't know that for sure," said Mrs. Newton. "You don't know that he's a bad man."

"Well," said Emily stoutly, "he let the puppies escape, didn't he?"

Mr. and Mrs. Newton had to admit that the little girl's logic was flawless.

Varnick was anxious to use the phone because he wanted to get ahold of his old henchmen, Vernon and Harvey. They had been in prison too, but had gotten out before Dr. Varnick because his crime was considered worse than theirs.

Vernon was happy to hear from his old boss, but Harvey wasn't.

"I want you to get up here right away," said Varnick. "I've located the people who put us in prison. It's payback time."

"I don't know, Boss, I don't want to get in any trouble. The last time I listened to you, I ended up in prison. And I didn't like it."

"Nothing is going to happen," said Varnick. "Just let me do the thinking for all of us, okay?"

"I dunno . . . ," said Harvey reluctantly.

"Just get up here. Hurry up."

The leader of the pack— Beethoven!

The only way to tell Dolly apart from her brothers is this big pink bow.

Beethoven and Missy *try* to keep a sharp eye on their brood.

Dolly, Tchaikovsky, Chubby and Moe.

If the pups
were bigger
they could do
so much more…

Trying to hide
with four on a
leash is hard work.

Half the litter
on the way
to the doghouse.

Beethoven's puppies!

Chapter Fourteen

THE PUPPIES' FIRST NIGHT IN THE WILD WAS BEGINNING TO fall, the sky darkening as the sun began to set. Moe had urged them on for most of the day, pushing them through the rough ground. They couldn't be sure how far they had gone, but they knew they were far away from Puppy Boot Camp.

"When are we going to stop?" asked Dolly plaintively. "I'm so tired I could fall asleep standing up."

"I'm hungry," moaned Chubby.

"I'm tired and hungry and thirsty," whined Tchaikovsky. "I think we should stop too."

"No," said Moe. "Let's try and go a little farther. We want to get home as soon as we can, don't we?"

"We're not going to get home tonight," said Tchaikovsky. "It's too far."

"And I'm hungry!" said Chubby.

Suddenly Moe stopped and peered into the gloom ahead.

"Finally," said Dolly. "Finally we can stop." She flopped down onto the soft pine needles of the forest floor.

"Sssh," hissed Moe. "I'm trying to hear something."

"What?" asked Tchaikovsky.

"Listen," said Moe. "Can you hear it?"

All four dogs were absolutely still, straining their floppy ears to hear the sound that had excited Moe so much.

"No," said Dolly. "I can't hear anything."

"All I can hear is my stomach rumbling," said Chubby.

"What is it?" asked Tchaikovsky.

"It's water . . . I can hear running water. I think there's a stream or a river up ahead someplace."

"Good," said Dolly. "Bring me back some water."

"Come on," said Moe. "Let's go till we find the stream. We're all really thirsty. It'll make us feel better if we get something to drink."

Even Dolly had to admit that Moe's plan made sense. With a groan she staggered to her feet and followed her brothers and sisters. "Okay," she said unhappily. "Let's get this over with, okay?"

The last few hundred yards were the hardest of the day. It was dark and chilly and the ground was rough and craggy and the land sloped downward sharply into the gorge containing the stream.

Moe was in the lead as usual, but even he found the going tough. He stumbled over some loose stones, lost his footing and tumbled forward into the darkness.

"Help!" yelped Moe.

"Moe!" shrieked the puppies in unison.

They heard Moe tumble down the slope, followed by a loud splash. Moe had somersaulted into the icy waters of the stream. He could feel the strong current of the torrent as it pulled him downstream and he tumbled end over end. Moe's legs flailed as he struggled to get in control, but he was so tired that he was having a hard time keeping his head above water. He could hear the other dogs barking and crying. It made him realize that he *had* to save himself because he was the only one who could lead his brothers and sisters out of the forest.

Moe summoned up the last of his remaining strength and paddled hard with his front paws, pushing himself out of the main part of the stream. Suddenly, he found that his back legs could touch bottom and he thrust down hard, throwing himself up on the riverbank. He lay there, panting hard, his heart beating fast. Then the cold set in and he started shivering.

Dolly, Tchaikovsky and Chubby gathered around him, yapping and barking, jumping with joy that Moe had managed to save himself.

"Moe! Moe! Are you all right?"

"Are you hurt?"

"Speak to us!"

Slowly, Moe got to his feet and shook the water from his fur. "I'm freezing," he said, shivering. The other dogs snuggled around him and tried to get him warm.

And that's how they fell asleep, cold and tired on the riverbank. Chubby didn't even complain about being hungry.

No one slept well in the Newton household. It took a long time for Mrs. Newton to get Emily settled down, she was so upset by the news of the puppies' flight. She couldn't stop thinking of the poor little dogs out in the cold night, hungry and thirsty. She insisted that Beethoven and Missy sleep in her room, to be close to her.

Ted and Ryce tossed and turned all night too, the worry about the puppies crowding sleep from their heads.

Alice Newton was disturbed by the effect the disappear-

ance was having on her children, and she told her husband
so.

"We have to do something, George," she said. "The kids
are so upset. I'm worried about them."

George Newton nodded. "I know. I know. But what can
we do? Colonel Happer said he would handle it. We don't
know the first thing about those woods. What good could
we do up there? We'd only be in the way."

"I think it would make the kids feel better. Emily was so
disturbed I was afraid she wouldn't go to sleep at all."

Mr. Newton sighed heavily. "This is getting out of hand.
If we hadn't kept the puppies, we wouldn't be in this
position. I was against it from the start. But would anyone
listen to me? No, of course not."

"It's too late for that, George," said Mrs. Newton sternly.
"We are in this position and we have to deal with it now."

"I suppose . . ."

"So what are you going to do about it?"

"Me? Why is it always me?"

"Because you're the head of the family. At least, that's
what you always tell me, isn't it?"

George Newton sighed heavily again. "Okay, okay . . .
I'll talk to Happer tomorrow. If he thinks it would do any
good, then we'll drive up there."

"That's not good enough," said Alice. "The kids have to
feel as if they're involved, as if they are *doing* something to
help their little furry friends. Whether they find them or not,
at least they have to have an idea that they tried. Do you
understand now, George?"

George Newton was silent for a moment, then he nodded
slowly. "I guess you're right. If Happer hasn't found them
by tomorrow morning, then we'll drive up there and take a
look around."

Alice Newton threw her arms around her husband and kissed him warmly. "I knew there was a reason I loved you."

"Because I'm a fool?" Mr. Newton asked.

"No, of course not. I love you because you always see reason in the end," she said. "Because you hate to admit it, but you always do the right thing when the time comes."

There were two members of the Newton household who did not sleep at all that night: Beethoven and Missy. The two dogs had understood the impassioned conversation over dinner. They knew that there was something wrong— terribly wrong—with their babies. The two big dogs knew what they had to do.

Once the house was dark and quiet, Beethoven and Missy got up from their place on the floor next to Emily's bed and silently padded down the stairs. Beethoven nosed open the back door of the house and the two of them ran out into the night, heading north for the mountains.

Walter Varnick knew it was time to go, to leave the Puppy Boot Camp behind once and for all. He waited until he heard Colonel Happer's long, deep-throated snores echoing down the hallway of the house, then he swung out of bed and got dressed quickly.

Tiptoeing down the stairs, Varnick paused long enough to lift the keys to the Colonel's beat-up old pickup truck and to take the few dollars that Happer kept in a cash box in the office.

Outside, Varnick slipped the emergency brake off the pickup truck and pushed it down the hill, rolling the vehicle a couple of hundred yards before he dared to start the engine. Once he was on his way, Varnick felt a great weight lift from his shoulders now that he was leaving the Puppy Boot Camp and its eccentric owner behind. It was like getting out of prison all over again. Suddenly, Varnick felt like singing!

Chapter Fifteen

THE PUPPIES AWOKE, COLD AND STIFF, IN THE MISTY GRAY morning light of the forest. They looked around themselves sleepily, sniffing the air and stretching their legs. The air was damp and dew dripped from the branches of the trees. There was almost absolute silence; the only sounds were the whistling of the wind through the trees and the constant sound of the water tumbling down the rocky stream.

"I'm hungry," said Chubby.

"We're still here," said Dolly unhappily. "I was so hoping that this was nothing more than a nightmare."

"I'm hungry," said Chubby.

"I'm afraid it's real, Dolly," said Moe.

"I'm hungry," said Chubby.

"What do we do now?" asked Tchaikovsky.

"I'm hungry," said Chubby.

"We have to go on," said Moe. "We can't stay here." He walked to the edge of the stream and took a gulp of the cold, sweet water.

"I'm hungry," said Chubby.

"We really should get something to eat," said Tchaikovsky. "We have to keep our strength up, you know."

"*Yes!*" said Chubby. "Yes, yes, yes, YES! Food. I need it. Gotta have it, lots of it and soon!"

"Well," said Moe, "we have to keep walking until we find some."

"That's it?" Chubby asked incredulously. "That's the solution? Keep walking until we find some?"

"You have a better idea?" asked Tchaikovsky.

Chubby's ears drooped and the little dog looked terribly sad. "No . . . No. I guess I don't."

"Then we better get started," said Moe.

"Which way?" asked Dolly.

Moe put his nose in the air and closed his eyes. There was something in his very core that gave him a natural sense of direction, a feeling that told him which was to go, that showed him the path home.

"Follow me," said Moe, leading the way. He started scrabbling up the hillside. Dutifully the other dogs fell in behind him, walking wearily toward home.

The sun was high in the sky when Moe stopped again. "I think we're near something," he announced.

"What is that supposed to mean?" asked Dolly. "No matter where you are you're always near *something*."

"No, no," retorted Moe. "That's not what I mean . . . I think we're near—"

"Food?" asked Chubby, her voice full of hope.

"Maybe," said Moe. "Up ahead, there's something there."

"What is it?" Tchaikovsky asked.

"I don't know," said Moe. "But it's there . . . Let's go find it."

*　　*　　*

The Newtons were up very early that morning. The three kids bolted down their breakfasts as fast as they could and were in the van before Mr. Newton finished his first cup of coffee.

"What's keeping them?" said Ted impatiently, bouncing in the backseat of the car. "How long does it take to eat breakfast? We have to get going. The puppies could be miles from the boot camp by now!"

"I'll get them," said Emily. She climbed over the seat and sat down in front of the steering wheel, then put all her weight on the horn. The horn blared loud, splitting the silence of the quiet suburban morning.

A second later Mr. Newton emerged from the house. "Emily! Stop that! You're going to wake the entire neighborhood."

"Come on, Daddy, let's go!"

"I'm not ready yet," said Mr. Newton. "As soon as I'm ready, we'll get started. Is that okay?"

"Well, get ready!"

"You mind your manners, young lady." Mr. Newton turned back toward the house. "And stay off the horn!"

As he walked away, Emily hit the horn again. Mr. Newton was so startled he jumped about two feet in the air. Ryce and Ted had to work to suppress their giggles.

"Emily!"

"Sorry, Daddy," said Emily innocently. "My hand just sort of . . . slipped."

Fifteen minutes later the family was on the road. "I hope this isn't a great big waste of time," grumbled George Newton.

"It isn't," insisted Ted.

"George . . . ," said Alice. "Remember what I told you. It's important to be part of the situation . . ."

"Right, right . . ."

Traffic was light that early in the morning and the Newtons were soon on the interstate highway, eating up the miles between them and the turnoff to the mountains.

"Daddy," asked Emily, "do you think the puppies are all right?"

"I'm sure they are, honey."

"And do you think they know that we're coming to rescue them?" the little girl asked. "I would hate them to think that we didn't care about them."

"I'm sure they don't think that, Emily," said Mrs. Newton. "The puppies know that we all love them."

"Did anyone remember to feed Beethoven and Missy?" Ryce asked suddenly. "I didn't see them this morning, did you?"

"They were in my room last night," said Emily. "But I don't think they were there this morning."

"I didn't feed them," said Mr. Newton.

"Neither did I," said Ted.

"I don't think anybody did," said Mrs. Newton.

The family was silent for a moment, then Emily's little face seemed to crumple as she started to cry. "Oh, no!" she sobbed. "Missy and Beethoven have left us too!"

Chapter Sixteen

"**O**H, HONEY!" MRS. NEWTON HALF TURNED IN THE front seat and patted her young daughter on the knee. "Don't cry. Please don't cry."

"But . . . but . . ." Emily could barely get the words out. "We used to have six dogs and now we have none!"

"Emily," said Ryce. "I'm sure that Beethoven and Missy are at home. We just didn't notice them this morning, that's all."

"We were in such a rush," said George Newton. "It's possible we just didn't see them, honey."

"They're gone," Emily wailed. "I know they're gone . . ."

George Newton hated to hear any of his children in such pain. "Don't worry, honey," he said. "We're going to find them all. That's a promise."

Emily managed to stop crying for a moment. "Daddy, do you mean that? Or are you just saying that to make me stop crying?"

"I mean it, honey. Honestly, I do."

"Really?" Emily's face seemed to brighten a bit.

"Really," said Mr. Newton.

Mrs. Newton glanced sideways at her husband. "Well, George," she whispered. "You've made the promise. I hope you can deliver on it."

It was a hard climb up, but Moe finally led his little band of dogs to the top of the hillside and found what they were looking for. It was the highway, eight lanes of thundering traffic racing in both directions. The four dogs huddled on the side of the road, scared by the roaring traffic and buffeted by the wind of the huge trucks that dashed by at sixty miles an hour or more.

"What do we do now?" Tchaikovsky asked at the top of his voice. "This is a dangerous place to be, Moe."

"I want to get away from here," Dolly cried.

"I'm still hungry!" said Chubby.

Moe stared at the traffic, looking to the far side of the road. "Do you see what's on the other side of this road? Over there, by those trees?"

They followed the line of his gaze.

"What? What?" said Tchaikovsky. "I don't see anything but cars."

All of a sudden Chubby shouted: "Hurray! I see it! And it is beautiful. We're saved at last!"

"What is it?" said Dolly.

Chubby could scarcely contain her excitement. "It's . . . It's a great big, beautiful overflowing garbage can!"

"Foooooooood!" howled Dolly. She started dancing around with Chubby. "It'll be full of food! You know how humans waste food! They throw everything away!"

"There's just one problem," said Moe. "It's over there—

and we're over here. How do we get to it? How do we cross the road?"

As if to underscore the difficulty before them, a long, long eighteen-wheel tractor-trailer blasted by, the roaring engine filling their ears. It seemed to make the air around them vibrate.

"Maybe we should just move on until we find something else to eat," said Moe. "We could get killed if we try to cross the road."

"No," whined Chubby. "No, no, *please,* no."

"So near and yet so far," whimpered Dolly.

"And we're soooo hungry," said Tchaikovsky.

"Well," said Moe, "do you want to try it? It's going to be dangerous, you know. But if want to risk it . . ."

"Sure," said Dolly. "You go first."

"No," said Chubby. "*I'll* go first."

"Save some for us," said Tchaikovsky.

Chubby took a deep breath and without looking left or right, dashed out into traffic! All of a sudden the air seemed to be filled with the sound of honking horns and screeching brakes as the cars and trucks veered and slalomed around the road trying to avoid Chubby as she made a dash for nourishment.

"I can't look!" shouted Dolly.

Chubby was running like a football player, dodging in and out of traffic, jumping, falling, rolling and then running again. More than once she was just inches from getting hit, but by some miracle, she managed to avoid getting splattered all over the road.

The little dog was panting with exertion when she finally crossed to the far side of the road, but that didn't stop her from running straight to the garbage can and knocking it down with her front paws. Trash scattered everywhere and to Chubby it all smelled delicious. She scrambled about in the mound of rubbish for a moment, until her jaws closed over something absolutely delicious!

Back on the other side of the road, the other three puppies watched enviously as their sister wolfed down some food.

"She's got pizza!" exclaimed Dolly.

"And there are bones there too! Sparerib bones!" howled Tchaikovsky enviously. "I have to go too!"

Someone must have had a roadside barbecue, because Moe could see that there were some half-eaten hot dogs and hamburgers scattered among the trash. He licked his lips and looked at the traffic.

"Well," he said, "if we're going to go, we might as well go now!" With that he dashed out into the road, the other two dogs right behind.

They were a little luckier than Chubby, as there was a slight lull in the traffic. In fact, the only thing coming was a dilapidated old pickup truck. But, unfortunately for the puppies, it was being driven by Varnick!

As the puppies dashed across the road in front of him, Varnick's mouth dropped open. Vernon and Harvey, crammed into the front seat of the truck with the boss, gaped too, none of them quite able to believe his eyes.

"Hey, Boss," said Harvey, "ain't them the—"

"Where did they come from?" asked Vernon.

Varnick stood on the brakes and the truck started to buck and swerve. The cars behind him started to skid and veer right and left.

"What are you doing?" Vernon yelled.

"I'm stopping," Varnick screamed.

"Noooooo," shouted Harvey. "Not here!"

At the last moment before there was a terrible ten-car pileup, Varnick stepped on the gas and looked to his left as he flashed by the puppies, who had made it to the side of the road and were now falling on the garbage.

"I've gotta find a place to turn around," said Varnick through clenched teeth. "We gotta get them pups!" He pushed the gas pedal all the way to the floorboards of the old truck and the pickup bucked forward.

"Don't go so fast, boss," said Harvey.

"Shuttup," snapped Varnick. "That old fool the Colonel is probably out looking for them already and we can get way ahead of him, if we can just find someplace to turn this old heap around!"

"Boss . . . I really think you should slow down," said Vernon. "It would be a smart move."

"Shuttup, Vernon! How in the heck am I supposed to catch those darn pups if I slow down? I wish this jalopy would move a little faster."

"Boss?"

"Don't bother me. I'm thinking."

From behind the truck came the sound of a siren and a voice on a loudspeaker. "You in the pickup truck! Pull over!"

Varnick looked in his rearview mirror. A police cruiser was right on his tail, the lights on the roof flashing an angry red.

"The cops!" howled Varnick. "Why didn't you tell me the cops were right there tailgating me, you two nincompoops!"

"We tried, boss, we tried," said Vernon.

"Honest," said Harvey.

"Shuttup!" Varnick slowed down and pulled the truck over to the side of the road. "Let me do the talking, okay?"

The state trooper walked over to Varnick's truck and looked at the driver with distaste. Varnick smiled a big phony smile and did his best to look appealing.

"Is there a problem, Officer?" he asked, his voice sort of smooth and oily.

"Yes, sir, there is." He took out his summons book. "Are you aware, sir, that you were doing seventy miles an hour in a fifty-five-mile-an-hour zone?"

"Was I? Tsk, tsk, tsk, how careless of me. Well, I assure you it won't happen again. You have my word on that, Officer."

The state trooper ripped a ticket off the pad. "And here's a little something to make sure you don't forget, sir."

Back at the rest area, the puppies were eating as much as they could as fast as they could. Not one of them—not even Chubby—had realized how hungry he or she was until they finally found some food.

They devoured the discarded pizza; they gnawed on the bones and ate the cast-off hamburgers and hot dogs.

Finally, all of them, even Chubby, had eaten their fill. They rolled on the grass, taking it easy after their feast.

"Oh, boy," said Chubby. "That was by far the best garbage I ever ate!"

"I agree," said Dolly.

"I'm in the mood for a nap," said Tchaikovsky.

"Maybe we should move away from the road," said Moe. "People can see us here and maybe—"

"I like it here," said Chubby.

"Me too," agreed Dolly.

"Oh, Moe," said Tchaikovsky, "you're such a worrier. What could possibly go wrong now?"

Chapter Seventeen

WHEN THE NEWTONS PULLED INTO THE PUPPY BOOT CAMP, Colonel Happer was waiting for them. He was dressed in his fatigues, and clipped to his equipment belt was all kinds of military accouterments and tools. He had binoculars and a canteen, range finders and an entrenching tool and a big long bayonet, as well as a box of waterproof matches, a fishing line, two or three different compasses and a first aid kit.

Colonel Happer saluted the Newtons smartly. "I cannot tell you how sorry I am that this unfortunate situation has developed. But I believe that this procedure, which I have designated Operation Puppy Find, will be one hundred percent successful."

"Ah, Colonel," said Alice Newton. "I can't help noticing that you have a gun there on your hip."

Happer slapped the big gun in the leather holster. "That's right, ma'am. This here's a Colt .45."

"Is that strictly necessary?" Mrs. Newton asked.

"You're not going to shoot the puppies, are you?" asked Emily, alarmed. "Maybe they did a bad thing by escaping. But they just wanted to get home. That's all. I don't think they should be—"

"No, young lady," said Happer gravely. "I could never bring myself to shoot a dog. But I have a feeling there's another varmint out there in the woods, and if I meet up with him, I want to have my iron along with me."

"What are you talking about?" asked George Newton.

"Well, I woke up this morning and I discovered that my assistant had flown the coop. Must have been last night. He took the cash box and my pickup truck to boot. I rue the day I ever hired that man. He was bad news."

Emily looked at her father and mother, a smug look of triumph on her face. "Told you so, didn't I?"

"That's all very well, Colonel," said Alice. "But I would feel better if you didn't carry the gun with you."

The Colonel thought for a moment and then pulled the holster off his belt. "An officer and a gentleman never refuses the request of a lady."

"I appreciate that, Colonel Happer."

"Let me just lock this up. You should never leave a gun lying around, you know." The Colonel vanished into the house and returned a minute or two later.

"Okay," he said. "Let's get this search-and-rescue operation going before the trail gets any colder. Troops, follow me!"

An hour and a half later, George Newton realized that he had never been so miserable in his entire life. He was hot and tired and footsore; there was dust up his nose and sweat in his hair. The Colonel was older than he was, but he had set a pretty fast pace and all the Newtons had to scramble to keep up with him.

Every so often, Happer would stop and examine the ground and nod to himself. George Newton was puzzled by this because to him one patch of ground looked more or less like another—yet the Colonel seemed to be studying it as if it were a weighty book full of information.

"Yep, they were here. Probably yesterday in the PM."

"Are you sure?" asked George Newton.

"Of course I'm sure!" Colonel Happer barked. "I can track any dog anywhere anytime. Four Saint Bernard pups leave a trail a mile wide. I once tracked a schnauzer all the way across the Rhineland. That's tracking, Newton!"

"Oh, okay," said George Newton.

"Let's get moving. This ain't a walk in the park, you know. Move out!" The Colonel marched forward, the Newtons trudging along behind him.

Varnick took the ticket from the state trooper, cursing under his breath, and drove off, slowly, as if he were going to obey every rule in the highway code. But the instant the state trooper was out of sight, Varnick hit the gas and took off.

"Boss," said Vernon. "I think you're going to get in trouble again. You better slow down a little."

"Yeah," said Harvey. "I think he's right."

"Listen, I don't pay you to think."

Both Harvey and Vernon looked puzzled. "But, Boss, you don't pay us at all," said Harvey.

"That's right, Boss."

"Well, if I did pay you, I wouldn't be paying you to think."

"Oh," said Harvey. "Okay."

Suddenly and without warning, Varnick threw the truck

into a screaming right-hand turn, bumped over the median and started going back the way they had come.

"Boss!" yelped Harvey and Vernon.

"I want those puppies!"

"Yeah, but don't you want to be alive when you get them?" yelped Vernon.

"Just hang on!"

The four pups lay on the grass in the rest area, their bellies full of food, the warm sun beating down on them. For the time being they did not appear to have a care in the world. They were sound asleep and oblivious to the sounds of the traffic rushing by in both directions on the highway.

They didn't even notice when there was a terrible squealing of brakes and Varnick's stolen pickup truck came to a halt in the rest area. The three men jumped out and looked at the snoozing puppies.

"This is gonna be easier than I thought," snarled Varnick. "Like taking candy from a baby."

He turned and snapped out an order. "In the back of the truck there's a sack. Go and get it!"

"Right, Boss," said Vernon.

Varnick rubbed his hands and cackled. "Now I have those Newtons right where I want them!"

"Those sure are cute pups, Boss," said Harvey. "What are you planning on doing with them?"

Varnick cackled again. "I don't know, but it's going to be nasty. And you can quote me on that."

Harvey looked puzzled. "Who to?"

"What a dummy you are," muttered Varnick. He snatched the sack from Vernon. "Gimme that!"

He bent over and reached down for the first puppy. Unfortunately for him, the first dog he grasped was Moe.

As soon as Varnick's hand closed around the loose fur on the scruff of Moe's neck, the little pup woke up—and he could tell that the hand laid on him was not a friendly one. In a split second, Moe underwent a complete character transformation. His eyes went red and wild and he growled loudly, his lips curled in a vicious snarl.

He barked once—a warning to his siblings—and then buried his teeth deep in the soft part of Varnick's hand, the wedge of flesh between the thumb and forefinger.

"Yeeeeeooooooooooow!" screamed Varnick. He waved his hand around, shrieking at the top of his lungs. "Get him off me! Get him off me!"

But Moe held on tenaciously, his teeth clenched and as difficult to dislodge as a fish hook. He growled loudly and didn't care how much Varnick screamed or capered about; he wasn't letting go until he was sure that his brothers and sisters had escaped.

The other dogs were running around like mad, barking and yelping. Tchaikovsky nipped at Harvey's ankles, making the hapless man dance around trying to avoid those powerful snapping jaws.

"Help! Help!" screamed Harvey. "I'm being attacked by a savage puppy!"

But there was no one to help him. Varnick had his own problems with Moe, and Vernon had his hands full with Dolly and Chubby. Both dogs had fallen on Vernon, rushing at him, jumping in the air and snapping at his hands and face, as well as biting his ankles.

"These dogs have gone nuts!" Vernon squawked.

The pain in Varnick's hand had just about crippled him. He sank to the ground, whimpering and pleading with the puppy to unclench his teeth.

Moe could see that Varnick wouldn't be much of a threat

for the moment, so he unsnapped his jaws and barked excitedly.

"Come on! Let's go! Follow me!" Moe scampered for the underbrush that ran alongside the highway. The other dogs followed him, leaving Varnick, Vernon and Harvey sprawled in the dust behind them.

The four puppies ran as fast as they could, racing down the hill and back into the forest at the bottom of the deep ravine. When they could run no longer, they stopped and flopped down, their chests heaving with the exertion of their fast escape.

"That was close," said Dolly.

"I'll say," said Chubby.

"How did they find us?" asked Tchaikovsky. "Humans can be really smart, but they can also be really dumb too."

Moe's head was reeling. "You know what?"

"What?" asked Dolly.

"I *bit* a human."

Biting was considered a definite no-no in the Beethoven family. Beethoven and Missy had always taught their children that biting was something they should never, never do—never, that is, unless there was no other alternative.

"Do you think Dad is going to be mad?" asked Moe.

"Nawwww," said Tchaikovsky. "Don't worry about it . . ."

Chapter Eighteen

IT LOOKED LIKE SOLID GROUND—BUT IT WASN'T SOLID ground. One moment Mr. Newton was wandering along in the woods trying to keep up with Colonel Happer and the next he was—*Kerploosh!*—waist deep in a swamp!

Mrs. Newton shrieked when she saw her husband disappear under the dirty, smelly surface of the swamp, and the children ran to the edge of the quagmire, their hands outstretched to yank their father from the ooze.

Colonel Happer heard the splash too, but he didn't seem to be too concerned. "Look out for the swamp," he called over his shoulder.

Puffing and spluttering, Mr. Newton waded out of the swamp, rubbing the muck from his face.

"This is ridiculous!" he shouted. "I've had it with this! This is a complete waste of my valuable time!"

"Be quiet," said Colonel Happer. "You'll spook 'em."

"Who?" asked Ted.

"The puppies, that's who."

"We're searching for them," said Alice Newton, "not stalking them."

"That's right, little lady," said Happer. "I plum forgot."

Mr. Newton was so angry he jumped up and down, his feet squishing in his shoes as he did it. "Would someone please pay attention to me, please!"

Happer, Mrs. Newton and the children looked at him expectantly. "Yes, dear," said Alice. "What would you like to say."

"I'd like to say . . . *I'm leaving!*" He turned around and started marching back the way he came.

"Look out for the swamp," cautioned Happer.

"Don't worry," said George Newton. "I see it. I'm going to go through this clump of bushes." He pushed his way through the foliage, a few of the branches smacking him in the face as he went.

"George!" Mrs. Newton called. "Where are you going?"

"Back to the car. I'll wait for you there!"

"But you don't know the way!"

"I'll find it. Don't worry about me."

Mrs. Newton turned to Colonel Happer. "Please make him stop. He's going to get lost and we'll spend the rest of the weekend looking for him."

The Colonel drew himself up to his full height. *"Newton! Halt!"*

Mr. Newton halted in the middle of the thicket of bushes and turned around. "My mind is made up, Colonel," he shouted. "Don't try and change my mind and don't try to bully me. Understand?"

"Mr. Newton," the Colonel bellowed, "you will stay with this outfit! You will not desert your unit! Do you read me, mister?"

Mr. Newton's reply was inaudible, but his wife and

children definitely got the idea it was not for family consumption.

"Mr. Newton! You will stay with the unit because I am carrying the first aid kit," the Colonel bellowed.

"Now, just what does that have to do with anything?" George Newton yelled back indignantly.

"The first aid kit contains calamine lotion!"

"So?"

"So, Mr. Newton, you are at present standing in a huge patch of poison ivy!"

The puppies continued on their way, but they were getting tired again, walking more and more slowly. They were traveling along a trail, a well-defined path through the woods. None of them thought this was strange.

"I can't believe home can be so far away from home," said Dolly plaintively. "I feel like we've been walking for months already!"

"I know what you mean," said Tchaikovsky. "I wonder if leaving the Puppy Boot Camp was the right thing to do."

"We had no choice," said Moe. "That bad man was going to get rid of us before our family came back. We *had* to escape."

"I suppose you're right," said Chubby sadly. "I just wish I didn't feel so—"

"Don't say it!" said Moe.

"Homesick?" said Chubby.

"Well, *I'll* say it," said Tchaikovsky. "I'm hungry again. And I don't care who knows it either!"

"Me too," said Dolly.

"That garbage can was good eating," said Chubby sadly. "I wish we could find another one!"

"Well, you're in luck," said Moe happily. "Because there's a garbage can right up ahead there."

The four puppies stopped and stared. Sure enough there was a full garbage can twenty-five or thirty yards ahead of them.

"I don't believe it!" said Tchaikovsky.

"Are . . . are we dreaming?" asked Dolly.

"I'm not!" said Chubby. He raced ahead of the pack, his tongue hanging out, barking in exhilaration.

One good push and the trash can tumbled over, scattering paper and tin cans all over the trail. Chubby immediately started rooting around in the rubbish looking for food. She was rewarded almost immediately as her teeth closed around half of a discarded ham sandwich. A second later she was joined by the others, who went at the litter as avidly as Chubby.

Not one of the puppies thought it was strange to find a full garbage can out there in the middle of nowhere—who knew what crazy things humans might do?—and, of course, they did not know how to read.

However, if they had been able to read, they would have seen the sign painted on the side of the garbage can: "THIS IS YOUR NATIONAL PARK. PLEASE KEEP IT CLEAN."

Chapter Nineteen

THE PUPPIES DID NOT CARE ABOUT KEEPING ANYTHING clean—in fact, they were beginning to look downright bedraggled themselves. They had mud on their paws and their fur was dirty and matted, but that didn't bother them at all. The only thing on their minds right at that moment was having a nice, filling afternoon snack.

This trash can wasn't quite the horn of plenty that the first one had been, but there were some sandwiches and cookies as well as some potato chips. Not bad for a little pick-me-up.

When they had eaten every scrap of cast-off food, they felt strong enough to keep on walking a little bit more.

"We'll just go until it starts to get dark," said Moe. "Then we'll get settled down for the night."

It was amazing what a full stomach could do for one's state of mind. "That's a good plan," said Dolly.

No one bothered to look at the sky. No one noticed the angry-looking clouds that were beginning to form over their heads . . .

*　　*　　*

Mr. Newton was covered in calamine lotion from head to toe, looking like a pink ghost. Unfortunately, Colonel Happer hadn't been too careful about keeping his first aid kit up to date, so the lotion was not as potent as it should have been. So George Newton could feel the itching on his face, his legs, his arms and his hands. It was all he could do to prevent himself from scratching his skin—the Colonel told him that it would only make matters worse.

"I will not scratch. I will not scratch. I will not scratch," he chanted through clenched teeth. "*I will not scratch!*"

The rest of the family was gathered at the living room window in Colonel Happer's farmhouse, watching the rain pour from the night sky. Every few moments thunder rumbled across the heavens and lightning shattered the darkness.

"I can't believe that those puppies are out there," said Ryce. "They must be wet and cold."

"And hungry," Ted added.

"The poor things . . . ," said Emily sadly.

"I will not scratch!" muttered Mr. Newton.

"I'm sure they're going to be all right," said Mrs. Newton, but she spoke with a certainty she did not really feel.

"Saint Bernards are a hardy, tough breed of canines," the Colonel boomed. "They'll know how to get dry and warm."

"I hope so," said Emily.

Mrs. Newton turned from the window and caught sight of her husband. "George!" she said, aghast. "You're scratching!"

"I can't help it!" George Newton closed his eyes and continued to scratch away. It seemed that this terrible day would never end.

*   *   *

When the skies opened and the rain started falling, all of the puppies woke up in an instant. In a matter of moments their fur was soaked and they shivered from the cold and in fear at the crashing thunder and the blazing lightning.

"Oh no!" Tchaikovsky shouted. "What are we going to do!"

"We have to find shelter," Moe replied.

The track they had traveled just that afternoon was fast becoming a rushing river of rainwater.

"We have to get to higher ground," said Moe. "Follow me."

The little dog splashed through the torrential downpour, scampering up the hillside, his paws slipping in the mud. The others scrambled after him and the four of them huddled in the lee of a rock, but they were still being lashed by the rain.

"This is no good," shouted Chubby.

"I want to go back to sleep," said Tchaikovsky.

"We *all* want to go back to sleep," said Dolly.

Moe stepped forward in the darkness, examining the side of the hill. "I think there's a cave up there."

"Let's go," said Chubby. "It'll be dry in there."

"Okay," said Moe, leading the way.

The interior of the cave was dark, but it was dry and appeared to be empty, although Moe detected a strange smell in there. The four puppies stopped just inside the cave and sniffed the air. Not one of them could identify it.

"What is that?" asked Tchaikovsky.

"I don't know," said Moe.

"Well, I know one thing," said Chubby.

"What's that?" asked Dolly.

"Whatever it is, you can't eat it." With that she found

herself a corner of the cave, curled up and fell asleep. Soon the other three puppies joined her and fell asleep too, as if they did not have a care in the world.

The first thing Moe noticed when he woke up the next morning was the strange smell was stronger. He got to his feet and shook himself and then looked around. The cave stretched far back into the side of the hill and Moe could not see much in the dim recesses. But he heard something . . .

From the back of the cave, Moe heard a deep, deep growl. Then it seemed as if the darkness in the rear of the cavern were moving. The growl got louder and louder until, finally, Moe was staring up into the face of an angry-looking black bear. The animal was eight feet tall, his paws had huge, long claws on them, and as the bear growled, he showed a mouth full of giant razor sharp teeth.

"Uh . . . Hi," said Moe as he tried to control his trembling. The bear snarled a little louder and looked at Moe as if he would make a nice little snack before breakfast.

The bear lumbered forward a few feet and let out a tremendous roar—a bellow so loud that the other three puppies woke up at once. The instant they saw the bear, they jumped straight into the air.

Before Dolly hit the ground, she started barking, a ferocious, high-pitched bow-wowing that gave the impression that if the bear were not very careful, she would be forced to do some serious harm to him.

For a second, the bear looked puzzled and not a little frightened by this sudden display of savagery. He dropped down on to all fours and backed up a few feet.

That was the break they needed. "Run!" Moe shouted. "Run! Now! Run as fast as you can!"

The other three dogs did not have to be told twice. They

ran down the muddy hillside, tumbling and somersaulting down the slope. The bear had recovered his poise and was standing at the mouth of the cave, thunderously bellowing his anger after them.

The dogs looked over their shoulders and saw that the bear did not look as if he were going to follow them. They slowed down a little, their hearts beating hard in their chests.

"Whew," said Moe. "That was close. You really saved the day, Dolly."

"I was so incredibly scared all I could think to do was to bark!" said Dolly. "I don't even know why I did!"

"Well, I'm glad you did," said Moe. "I thought that guy was going to eat me in one big gulp!"

"I'm tired of being out here." said Chubby sadly. "Let's get home!"

"Right," said Moe. "Let's go!"

Chapter Twenty

VARNICK, VERNON AND HARVEY HAD PATCHED THEMSELVES up after their painful encounter with the four puppies. Harvey's appetite for the chase had pretty much disappeared, but the suffering the puppies had inflicted on Varnick and Vernon made the two men all the more anxious to track them down and punish them.

"Those rotten little dogs must be running out of gas by now," said Varnick. "They can't keep this up forever."

"So where did they go, Boss?" asked Vernon. He had Band-Aids all over his ankles, but they were nothing compared to the huge bandage Varnick had on his hand.

Varnick spread a map on the hood of the beat-up old pickup truck he had stolen from Colonel Happer.

"They must be keeping off the roads," he said. "My guess is that they went into the national park." He punched a point on the map. "That's where we look next."

"Good," said Harvey happily. "I love to go to national parks. We'll see all kinds of animals, if we're lucky, and we can go see the geyser and—"

"Shuttup." Varnick snapped. "We're not going on vacation, you know. Now get in the truck."

Harvey's shoulders slumped. "Sorry, Boss."

Varnick started the engine and the old truck rattled all the way down the hill to the gate of the national park.

There was a park ranger waiting at the gate as the truck approached. She held up her hand and Varnick rolled to a halt.

"Good morning," the park ranger said. "Let's see, three adults and a vehicle . . . that comes to seventy-five dollars."

"Seventy five bucks!" screeched Varnick. "I don't want to *buy* the place. I just want to get in for a little while."

"Yes, sir," the park ranger said. "I understand that, but the entrance fee for three adults plus one vehicle is seventy-five dollars. The National Parks Service needs every penny it can get, you know."

"A penny I could live with," grumbled Varnick. "How much for two adults and a child?"

"That would be fifty dollars, sir."

"And how old is a child?"

"Up to thirteen years old, sir."

Varnick cocked a thumb at Harvey. "Yeah, well, he's only twelve. He's just big for his age, that's all."

"Good joke, sir," said the park ranger without laughing. "Pay up. Seventy-five dollars, please."

"Vernon," said Varnick. "Pay the man . . . I mean, the girl . . . I mean, pay the nice person."

"Why me?" Vernon protested.

"Because I don't have any money," Varnick whispered.

Vernon grumbled as he pulled out his wallet and carefully counted out seventy-five dollars exactly.

"I'd like a receipt," said Vernon. "I want to get my expenses back from my boss. This is a *business* expense."

The park ranger handed over a receipt. "Enjoy your stay in the park, sirs."

"Yeah, yeah," said Varnick. "Whatever."

They drove into the national park proper and put their Jeep in the lot. "From here," said Varnick, "we have to hike."

"Great," said Vernon. He was more interested in seeing if he'd get his seventy-five dollars back.

Harvey led the way happily. "I used to come here when I was a kid. Back when I was in the Boy Scouts!"

"*You* were in the Boy Scouts?" said Varnick.

"Sure I was . . . I got all my badges. When we get back to town, I'll show them to you, if you want."

"You don't gotta show me no stinkin' badges," said Vernon bitterly.

"Me neither," said Varnick. "All I want to do is grab those puppies, sell 'em and get out of town."

"I'm with you on that, Boss."

"But first we have to find those darn dogs."

They trudged around the park for quite a while—most of the day—but they saw no sign of the elusive puppies.

"Now, if you were a puppy," said Varnick, "what would be the most important thing on your mind?"

"I'm hungry," Chubby wailed.

"Again with the stomach," grumbled Tchaikovsky.

"I'm sorry, I can't help it. I have needs," said Chubby plaintively. "I need more nourishment because I'm so big boned."

"I wouldn't mind a little something myself," said Dolly. "It's been a long time since our last dip in a garbage pail."

"So what do we do?" asked Chubby.

"We look for food," said Moe.

They looked everywhere they could on the way. They even found a couple of garbage cans, but they didn't yield much, and by the time the afternoon came, all four dogs were very hungry.

"What are we going to do?" asked Tchaikovsky.

"We have to keep moving," said Moe.

The puppies plodded on a few hundred yards more. Then, all of a sudden, Tchaikovsky said, "You know, Moe, I'd like to know who appointed you the leader. You're always telling us what to do and it's beginning to get on my nerves."

Moe was shocked at Tchaikovsky's angry words. "I . . . I did what I thought I had to do to get us home."

"And are we home yet?" Tchaikovsky looked around. "Gee, that's funny, this doesn't *look* like home."

"I can't believe you're talking to me like this," said Moe. "I never wanted to be head honcho. It's just that someone needed to keep us moving along, that's all. Besides, it wasn't all me, you know. Dolly frightened off the bear. Chubby crossed the highway and found the first garbage can—"

"And we *all* got rid of the bad men," said Dolly. "Tchaikovsky, I think you're being a little hard on Moe."

"But he's so *bossy*."

"I didn't mean to be," said Moe, tears coming into his eyes. "I'm as hungry as you are. I'm as tired as you are . . . I'm as scared as you are. I want to get home too, you know. I want to see Mom and Dad and the family too. I wish we didn't have to do this, but there was no other way. If we hadn't escaped, we would have been split up and we wouldn't have seen each other ever again. For our whole lives . . . Do you understand that?"

All four of the puppies stopped in the middle of the trail and looked at one another, downhearted and worn out by the events of the past few days. They all loved each other so much, but they were young and bewildered, torn from the loving embrace of their nearest and dearest, and they were completely at sea in a world they did not understand.

"If I've been . . . bossy, I'm sorry. I didn't mean to be. I was just doing my best, that's all."

"We understand, Moe," said Chubby. "You haven't done anything wrong. Believe me when I say that."

Moe shook his head. "It's just that Tchaikovsky seems to think that I've been throwing my weight around and I would hate to think that I've been a bully or a dictator or anything like that."

"But it's okay, Moe," said Dolly. "You know as well as anyone that someone has to be alpha dog."

"Tchaikovsky, will you say something to Moe?" asked Chubby. "We know that you're just tired and hungry. We know you didn't mean the things you said to him."

"And Moe do you promise that you won't be angry at Tchaikovsky?" asked Dolly. "We wouldn't have gotten this far without you—both of you."

Tchaikovsky and Moe looked sidelong at each other, then looked away. Both of them were embarrassed by this sudden confrontation.

"Well," said Moe after a moment or two, "I'm not angry if he isn't."

"I guess . . . Me neither," said Tchaikovsky. "Moe, I'm sorry. I guess all the problems had been bothering me more than I thought."

"Well," said Moe reassuringly. "I think we're almost out of the woods. I can feel that it's not all that far to home."

"From here on it's plain sailing," said Dolly, suddenly feeling very upbeat and optimistic.

"Right," said Chubby happily. "We'll be home soon with Mom and Dad and Ted and Emily, Ryce, Mr. Newton, Mrs. Newton, and they'll make us lots of really, really delicious things to eat. More than we've ever had before in our lives!"

"Yeah!" said Tchaikovsky. "Our troubles are almost over. We've come this far, we can go the distance."

"Absolutely," said Moe. "Let's go. All of you—" Then he stopped and looked at his brother Tchaikovsky. "You say it."

"Follow me!" exclaimed Tchaikovsky.

"*Got you! Got you, you little rat dogs!*" Varnick was standing directly in front of them on the trail. He clapped his hands together and rubbed them luridly, leering down at the little dogs.

"Eek!" screamed Chubby.

"Run!" shouted Moe.

The four puppies whipped around and looked down the trail. Standing behind them were Harvey and Vernon, their arms outstretched, ready to catch the dogs if they tried to run away.

"Oh, no!" yelped Dolly.

"I think your time is up, little dogs," snarled Varnick. "You might as well come quietly. No trouble, now."

The puppies looked from Harvey to Vernon to Varnick and realized that the game was finally over. They were all on the verge of tears.

All of a sudden the whole scene was bathed in a quick flash of blinding white light, a light like lightning.

Chapter Twenty-One

"**A**WWW, LOOK, KIDS! THESE HERE ARE SAVAGE SAINT Bernards. They live in the wild and grow up to be big ol' wild Saint Bernards."

The four dogs and the three humans looked up and saw a huge, muscled man looking down at them. He had a camera around his thick neck and he snapped a few more pictures in the few seconds that everyone stood rooted in place. Behind the man were two children—a boy and a girl—gaping at the dogs.

"They don't look savage to me," said the boy. He was a towheaded boy of about thirteen years.

"That's right," said the girl. "There isn't any such thing as a wild Saint Bernard dog."

"Well, yes, there is," the man insisted. "If they aren't wild, then what are they doing here in a national park? There's nothing but wild animals in a national park, right? Look at these three guys here." He pointed to Varnick, Vernon and Harvey. "They are paralyzed with fear. Plain and simple."

"They're not anything but a bunch of puppies," insisted the little girl. "I'm not scared of them." The girl rummaged in the bag she carried over her shoulder and pulled out a cookie, then stepped forward and gathered Chubby up in her arms. Chubby jumped into her welcoming embrace, licked her face and gobbled down the cookie.

"See," said the girl. "This little puppy isn't dangerous. She's just a little bit hungry, that's all."

"A little bit! I'm a lot more than a little bit! Yes! Yes! Yes!" panted Chubby. "I'm hungry! I'm hungry! I'm hungry! *Feeeed* me, please. Feed me!"

"Look out, Maggie, that dog could maul you something awful! Next thing you know it'll turn on you—then where will you be?" The man looked ready to take to his heels if Chubby so much as growled.

"There's nothing savage about this dog," said Maggie in disgust. "This is just a little puppy."

The man peered at the little girl and the dog. "You sure you're okay with that vicious critter?"

"She's about as vicious as a bunny rabbit," said Maggie. "Isn't that right, girl?"

"That's right! That's right!" said Chubby. "I wouldn't hurt a fly!"

"You know," barked Moe, "Chubby may be on to something here. These people could get us out of here."

"You're absolutely right," said Tchaikovsky. He immediately raced up to one of the kids in the party and started jumping up excitedly. The boy scooped up the dog and held him close. "Hey, fella, how ya doin'?"

"Fine, really fine, "Tchaikovsky yammered. "I'm doing fine, but would you please do me a favor and get me out of here?"

"I'll bet you're hungry, boy," said the little kid. "Aren't you?"

"Well," barked Tchaikovsky, "now that you mention it, I think I am just the little bit peckish."

"You want something to eat, boy?"

"Well, I really hate to be forward," Tchaikovsky yapped. "But I wouldn't mind a morsel if you should happen to have one on you."

"Maggie," the boy shouted. "Give me a cookie for this little dog here, okay? Come on, hand it over."

The little girl threw a cookie to her brother, who fed it to Tchaikovsky. "There you go. Good, isn't it?"

Tchaikovsky gobbled it down and then licked his lips. "That was terrific! More! More! More!"

The other two puppies gathered around the children, yapping and begging for cookies and attention. The father of the two kids was hopping around taking pictures of his offspring posing with the four dogs. Everyone was ignoring Varnick and his henchmen, who were watching, feeling a little bewildered at this turn of events.

"What do we do, Boss?" Vernon whispered.

"We can't grab 'em while the tourists are around," said Varnick. "They'll report us to one of the park rangers. Besides, look at the size of that guy. I don't want to get into a fight with him, do you?"

"Nope," said Vernon.

The huge man was still clicking away happily and the puppies were doing their best to look as cute as they possibly could. They knew they were safe as long as they were with this family.

"Ooops," said the father. "That was my last picture. We should be moving on . . . it's getting late."

"Awww, Dad." said Maggie. "Can't we take them with us?"

"Sorry, honey. No can do. Mom wouldn't appreciate it if we came home from the park with a pack of wild Saint Bernards."

"Take us with you!" said Moe. "Please take us with you!"

"They're not wild!" Maggie insisted.

"Well, it doesn't matter," said her father. "Let's get going . . ."

"Okay . . . ," the boy said reluctantly.

The boy and girl and their father started walking down the trail toward the parking lot, the puppies scurrying along with them.

"They're getting away," grumbled Vernon.

"I know, I know," said Varnick.

The instant the puppies were out of the gate of the park, they glanced back at Varnick and then looked at one another.

"Time to go," said Moe.

"Right," agreed Chubby.

"Bye, kids," said Tchaikovsky. The four dogs scampered across the parking lot and into the underbrush beyond the gate to the park. In an instant they were gone.

"What was that all about?" Maggie wondered aloud.

"Told you they belonged in the wild," said her father. "Now maybe you'll believe your old man once in a while."

A second later Varnick, Vernon and Harvey went thundering by, running as fast as they could for the spot where the puppies had vanished. Maggie, her brother and father watched them go, completely bewildered by this sudden odd behavior by men and beasts.

"This is one wacky national park," said the man.

Chapter Twenty-Two

THE ATMOSPHERE IN THE NEWTON CAR WAS PROFOUNDLY SAD as they drove away from the Puppy Boot Camp. Colonel Happer had insisted that they stay and do another day's searching, but George and Alice Newton had vetoed the plan.

"If I go out there again," said Mr. Newton, "I'll end up breaking my neck. I still itch like crazy."

"Besides," said Mrs. Newton, "I think that Colonel Happer will do better without us, don't you?"

"No!" insisted Ted. "We have to find them!"

"That's right," said Emily firmly. "We can't give up now."

Mr. and Mrs. Newton exchanged a worried glance, then both of them reached down and embraced their children.

"Honey," said Mrs. Newton softly. "I think it's time to face the possibility that the puppies might be gone . . ."

They traveled many miles before anyone said anything. Finally, Mr. Newton broke the silence.

"Would anyone like to sing a song?" he asked with a forced joviality. "How about 'A Hundred Bottles of Beer on the Wall!'"

"No," said Emily.

"I'm not in the mood," said Ted.

"Me neither," Ryce mumbled.

"Oh . . . Okay," said Mr. Newton. They drove a few more miles in silence, then George Newton made another effort to lift the spirits of his family.

"You know, vacation time is coming up and I was thinking of renting a boat," he said. "Rent a big cabin cruiser and go sailing."

This announcement did arouse a certain amount of interest. Mrs. Newton looked at her husband as if he had suddenly taken leave of his senses.

"You were thinking of doing what?" she asked.

"Don't you think that's a good idea? Kids? What do you think?" Mr. Newton glanced in the rearview mirror, hoping he would see three beaming faces. Instead, they looked only mildly curious about their father's vacation plans.

"Could we take Beethoven and Missy and the puppies?" asked Emily

"Of course," said Mr. Newton. "If the puppies come back, we'll take all the dogs." He felt as if he were on pretty safe ground in saying that, because he was *sure* the puppies were finally gone for good.

Emily brightened considerably. "Really? You mean it?"

"Absolutely!" George Newton said forcefully.

"There you go making promises you can't keep," Mrs. Newton cautioned. "Watch what you say. Emily is like an elephant. She never forgets a thing."

"Promise, Daddy?" Emily pressed.

"I promise," said Mr. Newton.

"Cross your heart?"

Solemnly, Mr. Newton crossed his heart. "There," he said to his daughter. "Feel better now?"

"A little," said Emily with a smile.

"Then it was worth it," said Mr. Newton happily, pleased with his ability to cheer up his youngest child.

The puppies ran as fast as they could, but they were too tired to run for very long. Dolly was terribly winded.

"Can't we stop, please?" she said, panting hard. "Not even for minute or two so I can catch my breath?"

"But they could be somewhere behind, still chasing us," said Moe. "I don't think we can risk it."

"I have to stop too," said Tchaikovsky.

"Me too," admitted Chubby.

The four dogs slowed down, going from a gallop to a trot. Then they stopped altogether, dropping down on the warm ground.

"We can't just lie here," said Moe urgently. "We have to hide!"

"Where?"

"Let's get behind those rocks over there," suggested Chubby.

"Okay," said Moe. The four puppies scurried across the clear and darted behind a clump of boulders. They pressed up against the cold stone, trying to make themselves as still as possible. Their ears went up when they heard the sound of someone thrashing through the undergrowth and the angry voices of the three men.

"I am sick of looking for these darn puppies," grumbled Vernon. "They're only dogs, after all."

"Dogs, nothing," said Varnick. "They're more than that. They're the instruments of my revenge!"

"Sheesh, Boss," said Vernon, looking at Varnick worriedly. "You aren't going ding-a-ling on us, are you?"

"Don't be ridiculous . . . And if you don't care about revenge, then you better care about finding those puppies anyway."

"How come?" Vernon asked.

"Because if I don't get hold of those mangy little muts, you're not going to see your seventy-five bucks again. Understand?"

"Oh," said Vernon. "If you put it that way. Harvey!"

"What, Vern?"

"Get busy finding those four dogs!"

"Spread out," Varnick ordered. "We're not going to find them if we're all bunched up like this."

Vernon and Harvey took opposite sides of the clearing, while Varnick lowered himself onto the boulders and exhaled heavily, mopping his brow with a handkerchief. The puppies were just inches from him and they could smell him clearly, and it was not a smell they cared for in the least.

"Why does life have to be so hard?" Varnick said aloud.

None of the four dogs felt the slightest bit sorry for the man. And because they were so close to him, they were all thinking the same thing—they were all wondering just how sweet it would be to take a great big bite out of Varnick's behind.

"Found anything?" Varnick shouted to his two henchmen.

"Nope," Vernon called.

"Not yet, Boss," Harvey shouted back.

"Keep looking," Varnick commanded. "Those dogs have to be around here someplace or other."

All of a sudden, Tchaikovsky threw his head back and sneezed! It was the loudest sneeze any of the puppies had ever heard and it came at precisely the worst possible moment.

"Gezundheit!" said Varnick without thinking. He paused a moment and the puppies held their breath, hoping against hope that Varnick would not notice them crouched there. Then he shook his head as if checking what he had heard.

Varnick looked down and his eyes grew wide. "*You!*" he screamed.

Chubby didn't hesitate. She bit Varnick hard on his seat, then the four of them took off, running as fast as they had ever run before.

Chapter Twenty-Three

VARNICK SCREAMED IN AGONY, HOLDING ONTO HIS BEHIND and hopping around. "*Vern! Harvey! Owww! Over here! Yeowww!*"

"What's the matter with the boss?" Harvey asked, puzzled by Varnick's sudden and very strange behavior.

"I don't know," said Vernon, just as puzzled as his partner. "Maybe he got stung by a bee or something."

"*I said get over here!*" Varnick's face was red with rage and he was still capering around like a madman.

"We better get over there," said Harvey. The two men ran over to Varnick and tried to help.

"Did you get stung by a bee, Boss?" Vernon asked.

"You have to make sure that the stinger is out," said Harvey. "If you don't get the stinger out, it'll hurt for hours and hours."

"I didn't get stung!" Varnick screamed. "I was bitten!"

"No, no," said Harvey. "Bees don't bite. They sting."

"I know that, you moron! I got bit by a dog! I got bit by

one of *the* dogs, you numskulls. The ones we're looking for."

"Where? Where?" said Vernon.

"Where are they?" said Harvey, looking around.

"They're gone!" Varnick let go of his smarting behind long enough to point in the direction the dogs had fled. "That way! They ran toward the outskirts of town."

"Let's go!" shouted Vernon. "We're going to get them this time. You can bet on it, Boss!"

The two men led the charge, racing ahead of Varnick. They crashed through the sparse underbrush and ran across a field. A few hundred yards up ahead they could see the puppies running fast, but one of them—Dolly—was so tired that she was falling behind. She could feel her legs weakening under her, and her pace slowed.

"Dolly! Dolly!" Moe shouted over his shoulder. "Try and keep up! We're almost home! You can't stop now!"

"I can't," Dolly gasped. "I just *can't*!" She was almost crying, overwhelmed by her fatigue and her disappointment. She stopped and dropped to the grass and lay there panting heavily.

"Dolly," screamed Tchaikovsky. "Get up! Please, Dolly, please try to get up and run with us."

But Dolly was so tired it was all she could do to raise her head. "You go on ahead. I'll catch up . . ."

But Dolly and the other three dogs knew that was far from the truth. If Dolly stayed on the ground, then they knew they would never see her again and their long, painful quest for freedom would have been in vain.

The dogs stopped and looked at their fallen sister. Vernon and Harvey were whooping with joy as they dashed toward her.

"Got one!" howled Vernon.

"The rest will follow!" Harvey shouted.

He had no idea that for once he was absolutely correct. The two men bent to scoop up the worn-out puppy and then held her aloft, in triumph.

Tears streamed from the eyes of Moe, Tchaikovsky and Chubby. They couldn't believe that they had finally been separated.

Moe was so emotional he could scarcely speak. "We were born together," he said sadly. "We lived together, we escaped together . . . We have to stay together. It is our destiny to be together. I'm going to give myself up."

With that he started trotting toward Vernon and Harvey, just as Varnick came out of the thicket of trees, an evil smile on his face.

"Moe's right," said Tchaikovsky. "We belong together."

"That's right," said Chubby. "Let's go."

Together they followed their brother back toward the men who wanted to break up their family.

Varnick was beside himself with excitement. "Well, we finally nailed you four mutts. And about time too. I am going to enjoy my revenge more than you mongrels could ever imagine."

"What are you going to do, Boss?" asked Harvey. He was busy putting leashes on the collars around the dogs' necks.

"Medical experiments, perhaps." Varnick mused. "Maybe I'll see 'em to that outfit that trains attack dogs—you know how they do that, don't you?"

"Sure," said Vernon. "They starve 'em, beat 'em. They treat them rough until they're good and mean."

"That's right. It'll be a rude awakening for our little friends here. All they've ever known is love and affection. Well, that's going to change starting right now." Without warning, Varnick kicked the dog closest to him. Chubby yelped in pain and fear.

"And that's just the beginning," said Varnick, smiling that nasty grin of his. "Plenty more where that came from."

Vernon grabbed the leashes and yanked hard, pulling them back toward the path that led toward the pickup truck, still parked in the lot outside the national park.

"Man," said Vernon. "Am I happy that this thing is finally over and done with. I thought we'd be chasing these pups for the rest of my life."

"I know what you mean," said Harvey. He was silent for a moment and glanced at the four puppies.

The dogs walked slowly, their heads down, tears in their eyes and sorrow in the hearts.

"You know, I think the boss is being a little hard on these little fellas. Don't you, Vernon?"

"Nope," said Vernon. "Not me. If the boss wants it, the boss gets it. It's as simple as that. All I care is that he gets a good price for the critters and remembers to pay me my share of the proceeds."

The pups had never been so miserable in their entire lives. They couldn't believe that this had happened to them and they thought that their lives were over.

But all of that melancholy vanished when they entered the clearing where they had hidden from Varnick. Because sitting on the boulders, as if waiting for them to show up, was none other than . . . Beethoven and Missy!

Chapter Twenty-Four

FOR A MOMENT NOTHING HAPPENED. THE PUPPIES AND THE humans stopped and all seven jaws dropped open, as if no one could quite believe what they were seeing—as if Beethoven and Missy's sudden appearance were a mirage or an illusion.

Beethoven and Missy stared at their beloved children, relieved to see that they were alive. Tired and bedraggled though they were, the puppies were healthy and whole, and that was all that mattered.

Varnick, Vernon and Harvey could not believe their eyes. Of course, they all had met once before and there was no love lost between them. Beethoven's eyes seemed to drill straight into Varnick, and the big dog licked his chops eagerly, as if looking forward to what was about to happen.

Then everything changed.

From everything happening slowly, as if in slow motion, a split second later everything went to double time, just as if someone had put a movie into fast forward.

When all the connections were made in their various brains, the people and the dogs began to react.

First, the puppies, so excited were they at seeing their beloved mother and father, jumped straight up in the air and howled loud in happiness, elation, delight, delicious *relief*!

Second, Varnick, Vernon and Harvey could see the pure anger in Beethoven and Missy's eyes and realized that they were in deep, deep trouble.

Third, with two bloodcurdling snarls, Beethoven and Missy sprang off their perch, sailed through the air and landed on Varnick and Vernon, knocking both men to the ground.

Fourth, the puppies, all four of them, turned on Harvey and attacked.

Beethoven and Missy mauled Vernon and Varnick with their teeth and claws, punishing both men for their cruelty to the puppies. The hapless victims tried to push the dogs off, but Beethoven and Missy both weighed over two hundred pounds each *and* neither of them intended to let Vernon and Varnick go until their retribution had been taken. The three men flailed and floundered in the dust, yelling and shouting for help, but no one came to their assistance.

Finally, Beethoven and Missy backed off slightly and permitted Vernon and Varnick to stumble to their feet. The puppies took their cue from the parents and eased their attack on Harvey.

"You lousy dogs!" yelled Vernon.

"I'm gonna get you for this, you big mutts!" Varnick screamed. "This isn't over between us!"

A low, slow, menacing growl came from deep in Beethoven's throat. He bared his teeth and put his head down like a bull about to charge.

"You don't scare me." Varnick sneered. "The dog hasn't been born that scares me."

"Well, he scares me," said Vernon.

"Me too! You're on your own, Boss!" said Harvey. With that, both men took to their heels and started running away.

All four puppies chased after them and nipped at their heels, helping the two henchmen on their way.

Varnick decided he was going to leave with some dignity. "Lousy mutts," he muttered and attempted to walk out of the clearing with his head held high.

But Beethoven and Missy didn't want it that way. They roared like lions and chased after him, their jaws snapping at his behind like steel bear traps.

"Yipes!" shouted Varnick and ran like crazy, pounding out of the clearing in a cloud of dust.

When the men were gone, Missy and Beethoven turned to their children. With nuzzles and kisses, they told them they were finally safe, once and for all.

"The house just won't be the same without them," said Emily, sighing. The long ride was almost over and they were just a few miles from home.

"Try not to think about it, honey," said Mrs. Newton.

"That's not too easy," said Ryce.

"Right," said Ted.

"Maybe you should take your mind off it," said Mr. Newton. "Think about that vacation I told you about. Think about the great boat we're going to get. Try to look on the bright side of things."

He turned left onto their street, drove down the block and turned into the driveway. Mr. Newton stopped the van and then glanced at the porch of the house. His eyes widened and he couldn't quite believe what he was seeing.

"What the—?"

Emily sat up in her seat and her jaw dropped. "Puppies!"

There they were sitting in a row between Missy and Beethoven: all four puppies. They were dirty, they were tired, they were footsore—but they were home.

Chapter Twenty-Five

THINGS RETURNED TO NORMAL PRETTY QUICKLY. THE FIRST thing the Newtons did was give the puppies a big meal: cans and cans of dog food, followed by lots and lots of kibble, as well as all kinds of treats from the refrigerator. They put out so much food that the puppies couldn't eat it all—though Chubby certainly tried!

Then they got a thorough bath, with lots of soap and hot water. The puppies didn't enjoy that all that much, but Missy insisted that they get cleaned up. Then Ryce and Emily combed out their fur and dried them off with Mrs. Newton's hair dryer.

Then they played. For hours the children rolled and ran with the puppies and they chased one another all over the yard. Beethoven and Missy and Mrs. and Mr. Newton watched, with joy in their eyes, two sets of proud parents . . .

Finally, Alice Newton turned to her husband. "So, George, still plan on renting that boat?"

*　　*　　*

The house was still and quiet and everyone, human and dog alike, was asleep. Out in the street, the old pickup truck, Varnick at the wheel, rolled to a halt. He turned out the lights and got out of the truck, pausing to check the gun stuck in the waistband of his pants.

Neither Vernon nor Harvey was with him—they had made it clear that they were through with Varnick and had retired from the dog-napping business once and for all.

Varnick slunk up the driveway of the Newton house and crept across the porch to the front door. In prison, Varnick had met a burglar who had taught him the basics of lock picking, so he managed to get through the lock without too much trouble. In a minute or two he had the lock disabled and the front door swept open.

He smiled to himself. *Now* he would have his revenge. "There's no dog tougher than a gun," he whispered.

He skulked through the dark house, feeling his way from room to room, searching for Beethoven. He stopped at the door of the kitchen and listened—inside he could hear the deep snores of an adult male Saint Bernard. Silently, he pushed open the door.

Beethoven and Missy lay side by side, with the puppies snuggled around them. Varnick raised the gun and aimed right at Beethoven's head . . .

Then someone turned on the lights!

Varnick whipped around and saw Emily standing in the hall staring at him. To Emily, Varnick's face was something out of a nightmare.

"You!" she squeaked.

"Get outta here, kid!" Varnick hissed.

But Emily stood her ground. She filled her lungs with air and screamed one word: "*Beethoven!*"

Beethoven was awake in a split second, saw what was going on and leaped. His jaws closed around Varnick's wrist and the gun fell to the floor.

"*Yeowww!*" Varnick screamed as he felt his bones crack between Beethoven's teeth. "*Help!*"

Beethoven pulled the man to the ground and stood over him, ready to sink his fangs into Varnick's neck if he moved so much as a muscle.

The entire Newton family was pounding down the stairs. They burst into the kitchen and gaped.

"Emily!" screamed Mrs. Newton as she grabbed the little girl.

"Varnick!" shouted Ted. "It's Varnick."

"I thought he was in prison!" exclaimed Ryce.

"Obviously not," said Mr. Newton. "Alice, call the police . . ."

Varnick's voice was tight and panicky. "The police! Hey, mister, there's no need for the police. I didn't mean no harm. Let me go, okay? Just get this dog off me and I'll be on my way and you'll never see me again."

"Not a chance, Varnick," said Mr. Newton sternly. He looked down at Beethoven. "Beethoven," he ordered. "Sit!"

Beethoven lowered all two hundred pounds of his body onto Varnick's chest.

"Good boy," said Ted. "Now, stay!"

And Beethoven stayed there until the police came . . .